"You can't go around sticking your nose where it doesn't belong," Gabe said.

"No one else will believe Grams," Kristina asserted defensively.

"It's difficult to believe such accusations without concrete proof." He eased the car out of the parking lot and back onto the road leading to Boston.

"Well that's what I'm trying to do, find proof," she shot back.

"But you could get hurt."

"I didn't."

Gabe sighed. She touched his arm, drawing his gaze. There was no mistaking the sincerity in her eyes. "God sent you to protect me."

Gabe's stomach sank. "That kind of thinking can get you killed."

Books by Terri Reed

Love Inspired Suspense

Strictly Confidential
*Double Deception
Beloved Enemy
Her Christmas Protector
*Double Jeopardy
*Double Cross
*Double Threat Christmas
Her Last Chance
Chasing Shadows

*The McClains

Love Inspired

Love Comes Home
A Sheltering Love
A Sheltering Heart
A Time of Hope
Giving Thanks for Baby

TERRI REED

At an early age Terri Reed discovered the wonderful world of fiction and declared she would one day write a book. Now she is fulfilling that dream and enjoys writing for Steeple Hill. Her second book, *A Sheltering Love,* was a 2006 RITA® Award Finalist and a 2005 National Readers' Choice Award Finalist. Her book *Strictly Confidential,* book five of the Faith at the Crossroads continuity series, took third place in the 2007 American Christian Fiction Writers Book of the Year Award, and *Her Christmas Protector* took third place in 2008. She is an active member of both Romance Writers of America and American Christian Fiction Writers. She resides in the Pacific Northwest with her college-sweetheart husband, two wonderful children and an array of critters. When not writing, she enjoys spending time with her family and friends, gardening and playing with her dogs.

You can write to Terri at P.O. Box 19555, Portland, OR 97280. Visit her on the Web at www.loveinspiredauthors.com, leave comments on her blog at ladiesofsuspense.blogspot.com or e-mail her at terrireed@sterling.net.

Terri Reed

Chasing
Shadows

Steeple
Hill®

Published by Steeple Hill Books™

STEEPLE HILL BOOKS

Steeple
Hill®

Recycling programs
for this product may
not exist in your area.

ISBN-13: 978-0-373-44361-1

CHASING SHADOWS

www.SteepleHill.com

Printed in U.S.A.

Fear not, for I am with you;
Be not dismayed, for I am your God.
I will strengthen you,
Yes, I will help you,
I will uphold you with my righteous right hand.
—*Isaiah* 41:10

In loving memory of my grandmother Vida and my grandfather William.

Thank you to Sherry Mundt, Marketing Representative for SpringRidge at Charbonneau Campus, for answering all my questions and taking me on a tour. Any mistakes or liberties taken in this story are purely mine.

Also, thank you to my editor, Emily Rodmell, for her patience with me. I really appreciate you.

ONE

"People are disappearing!"

Kris Worth barely refrained from rolling her eyes. Her maternal grandmother had a flair for the dramatic, something that Kris had inherited, according to her parents. "Grams, what are you talking about?"

Sadie Arnold shut the door of her studio apartment in Miller's Rest Retirement Center and shuffled across the carpeted floor in her soft leather shoes to point one thin, shaky finger at her granddaughter. "I'm telling you, people are vanishing in the dark of the night."

Colored lights glowing from the small decorated Christmas tree in the corner cast a garish glow over Sadie, emphasizing the pallor of her complexion and making the elderly woman seem infinitely older than she had just two days ago.

Today was Sunday when they normally headed to the small community church at the nearby high school, but Sadie wasn't dressed for an outing. And there was no disguising that Sadie's shoulders hunched slightly more than normal beneath her powder-blue fuzzy sweater.

Her degenerative discs must be bothering her today.

Kris made a mental note to talk with the duty nurse about her grandmother's care. "You read too many murder mysteries."

Sadie waved away the comment. "First there was Lena Street. One night we're playing board games and the next day she's gone. And then night before last, Carl Remming was here with us, having some of Mrs. Tipple's delicious tea, and in the morning, he was gone, too."

Kris remembered Carl pretty well. He was a big man with a big laugh, who had done some time in prison when he was young. Gangster stuff, Sadie had whispered.

A tidbit Kris had kept to herself, lest her mother find out and then insist that Sadie move into a more "selective" retirement community. Something Sadie had fought against because she had no intention of rubbing elbows with "uppity people." Still, Miller's Rest wasn't exactly cheap.

As for Lena, Kris didn't have a mental image of the woman. "Maybe they passed on?"

Sadie shook her head and frowned. "No. They didn't die. They just disappeared." Sadie fumbled with the pocket of her sweater before producing a man's black wallet. "Carl wouldn't go anywhere without this."

"Grams, where did you get that?"

"I found it on the janitor's cart, hidden beneath some towels."

Kris couldn't believe what she was hearing. "What were you doing searching through the janitor's stuff?"

"Looking for clues," Sadie stated, as if it were obvious. "That janitor did something with my friends."

"I'm sure there's a logical explanation," Kris said in

a soothing tone, hoping to calm her grandmother's growing agitation. "Maybe he found the wallet on the ground somewhere."

Sadie pursed her lips for a moment. "I know what I know. Don't patronize me, dearie."

A smile tugged at the corner of Kris's mouth. Her grandmother had always been a pistol. While growing up, Kris had loved spending as much time with her as her parents would allow. "I wouldn't dream of patronizing you, Grams. I love you."

To prove the point, Kris rose from the edge of Sadie's bed and went to hug the only relative whose love she had never questioned. Sadie let Kris be herself. Kris thanked God every day for having blessed her with the best grandmother.

Sadie inspired a loyalty Kris didn't feel for her own mother and father, who wanted her to be a cookie-cutter, clichéd socialite. But Kris wanted more out of life. She wanted to use her talent as a photographer to glorify God, not climb the social ladder of Boston society.

Sadie patted Kris's back. "Don't get mushy on me, Krissy. It isn't polite."

Kris chuckled as she released Sadie. "You sound like Grandmother Worthington."

"Bah! Don't be rude," Sadie muttered with a grin.

Kris returned the grin. It was no secret that Emmeline Worthington and Sadie didn't mesh well. Emmeline thought her son had married beneath him and Sadie had thought Meredith married a stuffed shirt. The only thing the two older women had in common was their love for their one and only grandchild.

Sadie took Kris's arm and let Kris guide her to the oak rocker beside the window overlooking the lavish gardens, now dusted with a fresh coat of December snow, and spread across the back ten acres of the facility grounds. Trees lined the property, separating the retirement center from the Boston skyline. The township of Miller was a twenty-minute ride from Kris's downtown loft and another ten from her parents' Beacon Hill residence.

Charles and Meredith Worthington rarely visited, preferring that Kris bring Sadie to their home for occasional family dinners. Which, thankfully, were few and far between. Dinners with the Worthingtons were a case study in upper-crust dysfunction. Dress for dinner, no elbows on the table and certainly no talking about anything that even remotely resembled emotions. Something Kris had rebelled against most of her life.

After settling Sadie in the rocker, Kris resumed her spot on the bed, tucking her feet beneath her and gathering her long blond hair into one hand to lift the heavy mass off her neck. "What did Ms. Faust say about Carl and Lena disappearing?"

"Hmm?"

"You did ask Ms. Faust about them, didn't you?"

For a moment Sadie looked confused. "Them?"

Kris frowned. "Carl and Lena?"

Sadie's expression cleared and she scoffed with a gentle shake of her head. "That woman doesn't know her knee from her elbow."

"Grams," she admonished lightly. Admittedly, Ms.

Faust, the center director, wasn't the warm and fuzzy type. But she seemed well organized and competent.

Sadie rocked. "Carl would not go on vacation with his rheumatoid arthritis acting up the way it has been or without his wallet, and Lena hates going outside for anything, let alone a cruise. And for them both to go on vacation at the same time without saying a word to anyone is ludicrous."

The social butterfly of Miller's Rest, Sadie made knowing everyone's business her business. Kris didn't want to point out that neither Carl nor Lena needed Sadie's permission to leave the center, so instead she said, "I'm sure they'll return soon with plenty of stories to tell and Christmas gifts for everyone. And maybe Carl just lost his wallet."

Sadie's sparkling, dark blue eyes regarded Kris intently. "Is that what you'll be saying after *I* disappear?"

Kris blinked. Way, way too many mystery novels. "Grams, you are *not* going to disappear."

Shaking a finger at her, Sadie remarked, "Well if I do, don't be believing I went on vacation."

"Of course not, Grams. You wouldn't go on vacation without me," Kris quipped.

"Too true," Sadie replied. Then her brow furrowed. "I just think something has happened to Carl and Lena. Something bad."

"What can I do to ease your mind about them?" Seeing her grandmother so upset burned Kris's chest.

Sadie slapped her palm on the rocker's arm. "Call the police! Call the FBI! Find my friends!"

Kris could only think of one person who might be

willing to humor her by looking into the matter on the strength of Sadie's suspicions.

Gabriel Burke.

The man who'd broken her heart.

Homicide detective Gabe Burke hated the paperwork associated with closing a case. He wished the department would spring for a secretary to fill out the required stack of forms. And he made the suggestion every time he got a complaint about his illegible handwriting.

This particular pile of papers related to the murder of a prostitute by a john, who happened to be a married grade school teacher. Man, he hated cases like this. Just proved every human was capable of evil. With a grunt of disgust, Gabe gathered the forms and jammed them into the file folder.

His partner, Detective Angie Carlucci, stopped by his desk and regarded him with concern-filled dark eyes. "You okay?"

"Of course. Why wouldn't I be? It's Christmastime," he shot back, immediately regretting his harsh tone.

It wasn't Angie's fault he was on the brink of burnout. She was a good partner and friend. Though in those almond-shaped eyes he could see evidence of the signals she'd been giving off lately that she'd be open to taking their "partnership" to a new level.

No way. He didn't date fellow cops. He only dated uncomplicated women who didn't need anything but a good time. It was less emotionally taxing.

She shrugged and held up her strong, capable hands. "Just asking, Grinch."

"Sorry." He sighed. "This last case left a bitter taste."

"Yeah, I hear that." She took a seat at her desk across from him.

"Hey, Burke! Lady here to see you."

He turned his attention to the front of the station where Sergeant Sean O'Grady had called from, but was instantly distracted by an attractive blonde gliding toward him. His senses went on alert. She was stunning. Her long flowered skirt flirting around her knee-high leather boots and a ruffled blouse were more appropriate for an outdoor party than a police station in the dead of winter. A more suitable, cold-weather wool coat and colorful handbag hung over her arm.

Kristina Worthington.

What was *she* doing here? They hadn't talked in over eight years. He'd caught a glimpse of her at a friend's wedding a while ago, but he'd done a good job of avoiding her. Now she was in his place of work.

Not the typical Monday morning.

Gabe automatically rose as she stopped in front of him. Kristina regarded him with a mixture of wariness and hope in her baby blues. The top of her head reached his chin. He'd always been partial to petite women. This woman in particular.

Keep it professional, Burke.

"Kristina, long time no see. Can I help you?" he asked as he studied her beautiful oval face.

"I hope so." She glanced at Angie, who watched them with raised eyebrows. "Do you have a moment to talk?"

"Is this a police matter?" he questioned, ignoring the battering of his heart.

"Uh, well. Yes," she replied as a blush brightened her cheeks.

Now why did disappointment nip at him so viciously? He fought to keep his expression neutral. "Then we can talk here. This is my partner, Angie Carlucci."

Angie bolted up and held out her hand. "Nice to meet you, Mrs…?"

His unexpected visitor swallowed before reaching out. "Just Miss, Kris…tina Worthington."

Using her interrogation face, Angie hiked a hip on Gabe's desk and flipped her black ponytail over her shoulder. He smothered a grin at the display of female rivalry.

Kristina's gaze returned to him expectantly, probably anticipating he would fawn all over her as he'd done so long ago when he'd foolishly tried to believe in love and all the trappings that accompanied the sentiment. He'd made that mistake once. Once was enough.

Feeling the need to expedite things, he prompted, "What can I do for you?"

She twirled one long strand of silky hair around a slender finger of her ringless left hand. A monster-size emerald pendant hanging from her slender neck twinkled in the fluorescent overhead light. A blatant reminder they came from different worlds. "I know it's going to sound bizarre. I mean it's a strange tale and you probably won't believe me—"

He held up a hand, halting her as he pulled out a chair. "Here, sit. Just start at the beginning."

With a nod, she sat and waited until he was seated before launching into her story. She told them of the retirement center and her grandmother's insistence that people were disappearing. She was right. Her story did sound odd. Bizarre. And, yes, strange. But no worse than some of the stuff he'd heard before.

Life, he'd long ago acknowledged, was unpredictable. Anything could, and would, happen. Being prepared was half the battle.

When Kristina dug through her large tapestry bag and produced a man's black wallet, Gabe held out his hand. "You found this…on the janitor's cart?"

Kristina scrunched up her nose. "I didn't find it. My grandmother did. Hidden beneath a stack of towels."

He raised an eyebrow at that. "You two shouldn't be snooping around. You might actually find trouble." Gabe passed the wallet to Angie, who proceeded to pull out the contents.

"Driver's license. Expired," Angie announced. "Credit card, library card and a senior's discount restaurant card." She hopped off Gabe's desk and settled in her own desk chair. "I'll run these through the computer. See if we have him on file."

"You probably will," Kristina said. "My grandmother said he belonged to a gang when he was young."

"Then maybe he *wanted* to disappear?" Gabe suggested. "It wouldn't be unusual for an ex-gang member to need to vanish, if, say, someone he'd once crossed found out where he'd retired."

Kristina's eyebrows drew together. "I suppose. But what about Lena? She wasn't in a gang. She was a sweet little old lady."

"Maybe they ran off together," he remarked drily.

"Not according to the center's director." Blue fire sparked in her eyes. "Something's happened to them."

She seemed genuinely concerned. Gabe took out a pen and paper. "I'll do some checking and see if I can track Lena—what was the last name again?"

"Street."

"Right." He made a note. "And the janitor?"

"Frank Hayes," she supplied.

After jotting down the name, he asked, "Where can I reach you?"

The pretty blonde hesitated long enough to make him raise an eyebrow.

She surprised him further by taking the pen and paper from his hand with just the slightest brush of skin against skin, but awareness zipped all the way to Gabe's toes. He mentally shook the sensation off and focused on what she was doing. She wrote down her information and laid the paper on his desk.

Gabe sighed. "I'll let you know the minute I have anything," he said and motioned for her to proceed him. "I'll walk you out."

She didn't move. "Aren't you going to check into Frank?"

Slowly he nodded as a little bubble of irritation shot through him. He didn't need her dictating his job to him. "Yes. And I'll let you know what I find out."

She arched an eyebrow and crossed her arms over her chest, her tapestry bag dangling from the crook of her elbow. "I'd rather wait."

He shook his head. He'd rather she walked back out of his life, thank you very much. "That won't be necessary."

"I'll wait," she repeated.

Figured *Miss Worthington* of the Beacon Hill Worthingtons would expect to have her own way. Seems the rich, pampered socialite hadn't changed. Though she'd tried her hardest to make him change when they'd dated, wanting him to be more like the rest of the people in her privileged world, his world consisted of Good Will purchases and Top Ramen. Like water and oil. Their lives didn't mix well.

Angie turned in her chair to say, "Carl Remming is an ex-con. Busted at nineteen for shoplifting and again in his early twenties for grand theft auto. Has a clean sheet after that. I'll run his credit card."

Gabe nodded his approval. "Check with the airlines, buses, trains for both Carl and Lena Street."

"Righto," Angie agreed and returned her focus to the computer.

Gabe gave in and sat back down. "Are you always this tenacious?"

Kristina lifted her chin. "I find it helps in certain situations."

He met her gaze. Ah, there was the queenly stare he remembered so well. She was some piece of work; all beauty, brains and self-confidence. Lucky for him, she wasn't his problem.

She shifted her gaze to the computer. "I noticed Frank had on very high-end tennis shoes and a Cartier watch."

"The watch could be a fake," Gabe cautioned, annoyed that she'd assume a janitor couldn't afford nice things. "Or he could have saved up."

"Of course the watch could be fake." Her tone

matched his growing irritation. "It's just…well, you'd have to meet him."

If the man checked out, Gabe wouldn't have to meet him. He typed Frank's name into the computer. Kristina came around the desk to peer over his shoulder. Her fresh, powdery scent teased his nose and brought back memories he'd thought long gone.

He gave her a sidelong glance. "Do you mind?"

She had the grace to duck her chin sheepishly as she stepped back. He forced himself to concentrate.

Within a few minutes, a rap sheet filled with petty larceny and misdemeanor assault charges came up. Okay, so Frank wasn't a squeaky-clean janitor. Everyone had a past. But experience had jaded Gabe enough to know a criminal past usually never stayed in the past.

"So, he bears watching," he conceded.

An I-told-you-so look bloomed in Kristina's clear blue eyes.

"Well?"

"Well, what?"

"You're not going to at least question him?"

"In due time," he said, rebuffing her astounded expression. "First we have to establish probable cause to bring him in. And until we have more information about Carl's and Lena's whereabouts, I'm not jumping to conclusions."

"But he had Carl's wallet," she pointed out. "That can't be good."

Was she kidding? "For all we know, he found it," Gabe countered. "Now, if you'll excuse us, we have some work to do." He stood and pointedly waited for

Kristina to precede him. "I promise to call you the second we've found something concrete."

"Sure. Fine. I'll just sit by the phone and wait," she stated tartly before walking away.

Gabe had a bad feeling in the pit of his stomach. Kristina Worthington didn't ever sit around and wait. He could only hope she didn't do anything to get herself in trouble or interfere with his investigation. Or his peace of mind.

"Just sit by the phone and wait," Kris grumbled as she crouched behind a stack of crates at the far end of an alley in midtown Boston. "Fat chance."

Somewhere in the distance a horn honked. Otherwise, the streets were quiet and freezing. Late-night air seeped through her black jeans, black turtleneck and black parka. She'd bound up her hair under a dark baseball cap. Her ears were getting cold. Thankfully it wasn't snowing again. Her nose wrinkled at the many odd and unpleasant odors wafting in the air. She distracted herself the same way she had since the adrenaline rush of conducting her very own stakeout—by bringing her camera up to her eye.

The shutter silently captured Frank Hayes's every move. She'd been following the janitor for the past hour, ever since he'd left Miller's Rest in his little beat-up two-seater.

He'd eaten at a dive that served more booze than food before heading out the back door and down this alley.

Gabe wanted proof the guy was doing something he shouldn't; well, she'd give it to him.

I'm not jumping to conclusions, he'd said. He'd "watch" Frank, he'd said. Ha! She didn't see him anywhere around.

Why she'd ever thought herself in love with Gabe Burke she didn't know. The man was even more stubborn than she remembered. And he'd acted as though he hardly knew her. Hurt rubbed at the wounds left by the summer they'd spent together. Obviously, she hadn't meant much to him.

Well, good. He didn't mean anything to her, either.

And contrary to his wishes, she was going to find out what Frank was up to. Then Gabe would have to act.

Frank, his shoulders hunched beneath his big down jacket, turned the corner, disappearing from her view. Kris hustled closer, her black boots squishing in the slushy snow. She paused at the edge of a brick building and cautiously peered around to the other side. There he was, ambling down the deserted street.

Just as she stepped around the building, a hand closed over her mouth and a strong arm cinched across her waist.

Her muffled scream echoed in her ears.

Frank Hayes whirled around. Body tense, his heart hammered against his ribs as adrenaline rushed to his brain, making the world shift slightly. He could have sworn he heard the scuffle of feet on the pavement. The echo of a muted scream. He searched the inky street for signs of being followed. He was alone. Or was he?

He backed up a few steps before turning and hurrying to the end of the block. Just a little farther and he'd be done with his business. He shivered. He loathed being outside in the dark. Too many shadows, too many possibilities.

Bad things happened in the dark.

TWO

Kris clutched her camera to her chest and used her booted heel to kick the person holding her. *Please, Lord, save me!* She whipped her head around, trying to loosen the grip over her mouth.

"Kristina! Stop!"

The harshly whispered command given in a familiar deep baritone registered. She went limp with relief. The arm around her waist held her for a moment before withdrawing. She sagged, using the brick building for support.

Taking deep, calming breaths, she allowed anger to replace her terror. "What do you think you're doing?"

The moon bathed Gabe Burke's hard expression in the muted light. He'd changed out of his suit into jeans and a dark leather bomber jacket. A knit beanie covered his honey-blond hair. "I'm doing my job. What are you doing?"

"Your job." She pushed away from the wall. Anger warmed her face. Peering around the corner, she smacked the bricks with her palm. "He's turning the corner."

"You need to go home."

"No way." She darted forward. "We have to at least try to catch up."

Gabe gritted his teeth. Short of hauling her over his shoulder and carrying her away, he had no choice but to follow. Frank was probably gone now, anyway. Gabe would let Kristina figure it out and then he'd escort her home. Though he'd like nothing better than to throw her in jail for doing something as idiotic and dangerous as following an ex-con.

After Kristina left the station, Gabe had done a little digging and found out that Frank hung out at the HogsHead Tavern. And sure enough, Frank had shown up. Gabe had intended to follow him when he'd seen someone else doing the same. It had taken less than ten seconds for him to recognize the lithe lines of Kristina Worthington. The fact that he could still do so didn't say much about his ability to forget her.

He grabbed her by the elbow and pulled her out of the middle of the street and into the shadows where they would be less visible as they followed. Thankfully, this part of town quieted down at night. But in a few hours, when the bars closed, the story would be vastly different.

At the next corner, he pushed her behind him and looked down the street. The dim glow of the moon barely revealed Frank. Gabe debated for a second about lying to Kristina and saying Frank was gone, but lying never solved anything.

Besides, he had a strong hunch she would just do this again. And he may not be there to protect her.

Clutching her slender, cold hand, he pulled her

around the corner and kept to the shadows. Ahead, Frank paused and whirled around.

Gabe reacted swiftly, pulling Kristina into his arms and angling his body to shield her from view. Gabe bent his head close, suspended inches from Kristina's lips while keeping his gaze on Frank. He heard her sharp intake of breath.

The man either didn't notice them or saw what Gabe had intended, a pair of lovers stealing a kiss in the moonlight. Frank continued on.

Gabe should have stepped back, far away from Kristina right then, but she was so soft and pliant in his arms. Her sweet breath fanned over his face causing a yearning to kiss her lips that gripped him in a tight vise. And suddenly he was back to those warm summer days when he'd been a rookie cop wild about a girl way out of his league, yet sure a future together wasn't impossible. That maybe he'd found what his mother insisted existed.

But then reality had set in and he'd walked away.

And kissing Kristina now would only cause him more pain than he was willing to endure.

Using every ounce of self-control he possessed, he released her and stumbled back.

She blinked up at him with wide, confused eyes. "What was that?"

Refocusing on the situation, he put his finger to his lips. "Shh. We better hurry."

Taking her hand again, they moved forward, keeping close to the buildings. Up ahead, Frank slipped down a side alley. Gabe and Kristina ran for cover behind a parked car where they had a clear view of the alley. They watched as a man stepped out of the deeper darkness. He was of medium height and build with short cropped hair and a goatee on his pointed chin.

Kristina raised her camera.

"Hey, be careful," Gabe admonished softly.

"I will." She snapped some shots.

In the alley, Frank was handing the man an envelope. The man ripped the envelope open and spilled the contents into his hand. From this distance, Gabe couldn't see what had come out.

Just then, Frank spun in their direction, seeming to stare directly at them.

Gabe grabbed Kristina and pulled her into a crouch.

"I don't think he saw me," she whispered, her voice shaky.

Gabe clenched his jaw tight. He scrambled onto his belly and watched the two men from underneath the car. The two spoke for a moment more, then the man handed Frank something before Frank scurried down an adjacent alley while the other man disappeared back the way he'd come. Gabe listened hard, but he didn't hear a car engine start. Which meant no plates to run. He shoved himself to his feet and brushed himself off.

"Aren't you going to arrest him?" Kristina asked.

"For what? We don't have any idea if he's up to something illegal and I don't want to spook him. Let's see where he goes now."

Cautiously they followed Frank back to his little car.

"I parked over there." Kristina dug into her pocket for her keys.

Gabe took her hand. "We'll take mine."

He led her to his black 4x4. Once settled inside, he pulled out of his parking space and followed Frank's car onto the tollway back to Miller's Rest.

"Nice ride," she commented, her tone bland.

Unsure if she was mocking him or not, he said, "I like it."

"It suits you."

"Meaning?"

"All of our choices in life reveal a little about us."

She'd become philosophical in the past eight years. "And what does my rig say about me?"

"You like to be in control and have a lot of power. Black is the absence of light. It's mysterious, serious and dramatic."

He wasn't sure exactly how to take that. "And you know this…how?"

She waved a hand. "Just one of the many things I learned in college."

"Ah, yes." She'd been enrolled at Boston University when they'd met. He couldn't remember her major. "You a psychologist or something?"

"No. Just took some psych classes."

"So what color car do you drive?"

She gave a small laugh. "Oh, my car won't reveal anything about me. It's my grandmother's car."

He glanced sideways, taking in Kristina's profile, liking the straight line of her nose and the arch of her brows. Her cheekbones were high and her jawline strong yet feminine. She'd actually grown more beautiful over the years.

She'd taken off her black cap. Her long blond hair

fell over her shoulders, the strands illuminated against her black clothing.

Gabe slowed the car as Frank parked at the retirement center and hurriedly entered the facility through a side entrance. "Investigation's over tonight." Unless Gabe wanted to break in and follow, which he didn't. He made a U-turn and headed back the way they'd come.

"Did you find out anything about Carl and Lena?" Kris asked.

"Not yet." He put his hand on her shoulder. "This isn't some game, you know."

"I'm not playing a game," she said with a huff.

"You can't go around sneaking through the night like some superhero looking for danger. Eventually you'll find it, and then what?"

She batted her lashes at him. "I'll call you."

The mockery in her tone made his lips twitch but deep down he did want to be the one she turned to.

As she had today.

Pushing away that errant thought, he had to make her understand that putting herself needlessly in danger was *not* a good thing. "Listen, Kristina. I appreciate your loyalty to your grandmother and her friends, but you can't go around sticking your nose where it doesn't belong."

"No one else will believe Grams," she asserted defensively.

"It's difficult to believe such accusations without concrete proof."

"Well, that's what I'm trying to do, find proof," she shot back.

"But you could get hurt."

"I didn't."

Gabe sighed.

She touched his arm, drawing his gaze. There was no mistaking the sincerity in her eyes. "God sent you to protect me."

Gabe's stomach sank. "That kind of thinking can get you killed."

Through the slit in the curtains inside his apartment at the far end of the retirement center, Frank watched the dark vehicle's taillights as it left the parking lot. His gut churned. What should he do?

After turning on every light, he grabbed the phone and punched in a number.

A few moments later a groggy voice answered. "Hello?"

"It's me, Frank."

"Do you know what time it is? What do you want?"

"I've got a problem. I think Sadie Arnold's granddaughter followed me tonight. I think she saw me."

"Don't be ridiculous. Why would she do that?"

"I don't know," he whined. "She's been at the center a lot lately. I don't like the way she looks at me."

"Have you been careless?"

He plopped down on the old blue couch that had come with the room. "No." At least he hadn't thought he'd been. "What should I do?"

"Stop worrying. She'll be taken care of."

"She will?" Frank breathed a sigh of relief. He didn't have to do anything. "Good. Okay, good."

"Now, good night, Frank."

He hung up and hugged his waist, trying to settle the gurgling in his stomach.

The headlights of Gabe's SUV sliced through the dark to illuminate the road back into the city. Gabe glanced at Kristina's pale hand still resting on the sleeve of his jacket. His words hung in the air. He flicked a peek at her face and met her gaze. With the faint bit of moonlight, he could see the stunned concern in her expression.

"How can you say that?" Kristina finally asked, tightening her hold on him.

He forced his gaze forward to the road. "You can't count on God to send someone every time you get in trouble."

"I trust He'll provide what I need. Tonight, He provided you." She tapped his arm before withdrawing her hand. "God takes care of those who love Him."

He glanced her way. The earnestness in her expression made Gabe tighten his grip on the steering wheel. "You sound like my mother. She's always saying things like that."

"So I take it you don't believe in God."

Concentrating on the road ahead, he replied, "I don't believe in anything I can't see, touch, taste or smell."

"What a Doubting Thomas you are. Don't you put stock in gut feelings?"

He frowned. "Of course I do. I've had plenty and they've kept me alive. But that's not God."

"How do you know?" she challenged. "How can you be sure those feelings weren't God warning you?"

"I just am." He shifted uncomfortably in his seat.

Once his ex-partner, Brody McClain, had asked him the same question, right after they'd survived a shoot-out.

Gabe had felt something, an inner knowledge things were about to go bad, a feeling that had made him pull Brody back from the door just as the wood exploded in a spray of gunfire. The incident still puzzled him.

But God protecting him? No way. God hadn't been there when Gabe had been a child and needed Him. Why would God suddenly take an interest in him as an adult?

"So after college…what?" he asked, needing to change the subject. He hadn't divulged information about his childhood to her the first time around and he had no intention of doing so now.

"I'm a photographer and I love it." She shifted toward him, her face animated in the moon's glow. "I was fourteen when Grams gave me my first camera. I never went anywhere without that little Nikon."

"I remember." She'd carried the thing with her all the time. He hadn't given it much thought then.

"Drove my family crazy because I was always snapping off shots." She looked out the front window. "Every summer my parents sent me away to Camp Greenleaf. The only thing that made camp bearable every year was my camera and Meg McClain."

"That's how you two met?"

"Yep. *She* liked going there."

"And you didn't like camp."

She plucked at a wayward strand of hair. "Not really. I wasn't used to the rustic life, which earned me a lot of teasing."

"I can imagine," he murmured, thinking back to the

days they'd spent together. She'd liked restaurants and the ballet. He'd preferred sidewalk vendors and baseball games.

"What's that supposed to mean?"

He shrugged. "You're a Worthington. Used to the good things in life."

She sighed. "We're back to that old argument?"

"No," he stated firmly. He didn't want to rehash the past. "I saw the picture in the paper of the new hospital wing named after your family. Nice."

"Yeah, nice."

The derision in her voice made him curious. "You don't like hospitals?"

"I don't like my family putting their name on a building. It's too…"

"Pretentious?" he teased, expecting to ruffle her defensive feathers.

"Exactly."

Interesting. This was a different side to the woman he'd known. He pulled up alongside her car. "You've changed."

She titled her head, her hand on the knob. "Is that a good thing or a bad thing?"

"I'm not sure yet."

She laughed and stepped out. When she opened the door to her car, he called out, "I'll follow you. Make sure you get home safely."

"No need. I'll be fine," she said before slipping inside.

True to his word, Gabe followed her.

Kris thought that was sweet, really sweet. Her senses still struggled to accept how she'd reacted to his near-kiss earlier. One second they were following Frank and the next—wham. Gabe had been so close, she could breathe in his aftershave, could see the darkening stubble where his beard would grow in and his strong mouth drew her like a beacon on a stormy night.

And being held that close felt so…right.

Even more so than before. At age twenty, she'd been in awe of Gabe. He was older, handsome and the opposite of everything her parents expected for her.

In retrospect, his "unsuitability" had been part of Gabe's appeal. He'd been exciting, dangerous and forbidden. And for three glorious months that summer, she'd felt alive.

Until her parents demanded to meet him.

Then everything fell apart and Gabe had walked away, taking her heart with him.

She'd nursed her wounds while she finished her education and then finally decided she had to get over Gabe. She'd dated several attractive, appropriate men and had even become engaged to a nice man whom her parents approved of.

But she'd broken it off because even thinking about spending the rest of her life with Tom Roberts had given her anxiety attacks. Tom had liked her family's prestige and power too much and he hadn't wanted Kris to continue with her photography once they were married.

She knew then that she was done looking for Mr. Right. God was going to have to bring the right man to her.

She parked in her usual spot and got out, just as Gabe halted beside her and rolled down his window.

"This is where you live?" His dubious expression was priceless.

With a sweeping gesture at the two-story warehouse converted to loft apartments, she said, "Home sweet home."

"I'd have expected you to live in Beacon Hill near your parents."

She gave him a tight smile. "This is what I can afford and it's a safe neighborhood."

He leaned an elbow on the window ledge. "What? Mommy and Daddy don't pay?"

Anger swept through her. This was exactly why she went by Kris Worth for her professional work, because people like Gabe expected her to live off her parents. "No. They don't. Everything I need is close at hand. I have easy access to downtown and the park is within walking distance. And I have lots of space for my business. The other residents are a good group of people. We're very close-knit."

"Interesting," he commented with a bemused half smile.

Uncomfortable with the focus on her, she asked, "What are you going to do about Frank? And Carl and Lena?"

He shrugged. "Nothing tonight. I'll look into the situation more tomorrow."

At least he wasn't blowing her off. "Good. Let me know what you find," she said and hurried inside.

Before turning on her lights, she went to the front window of her living area. Gabe sat in his car, his gaze trained on the building. Probably waiting to see which floor was hers. If she didn't turn on the light, would he come charging up to see if she was okay? The thought intrigued her and made her heart pound. What would she do if he did?

She reached over to the table lamp and flipped on the light.

Gabe drove away. Yep, he'd been waiting to make sure she got into her apartment safely. A pleased rush filled her. It was kind of nice having him worry about her like that. Of course, he was just doing his job, she reminded herself. Protecting people was what he did for a living. She was just one of those people.

She took her camera to the back half of the apartment, which had been converted to a photography studio. She'd had walls removed, the floor redone with hardwood and had lighting equipment mounted in strategic places. The remodel had used her entire savings, but the space worked well. And she loved her life here.

In one corner was her processing station. Gabe may not think there was anything more they could do tonight, but Kris knew otherwise. She hooked up the camera to the desktop computer and downloaded the pictures she'd taken.

Within a few minutes she was viewing the shots of Frank and the mysterious man in the alley. She had a clear shot of Frank handing an envelope to the man. Another of the man sliding the contents into his hand. She zoomed the picture in.

"Gotcha!" she stated to the photo. With satisfaction and anticipation, she grabbed the phone and called BPD and asked for Gabe, figuring he'd be back at his desk by now.

She was told he was off duty. So he'd been investigating on his own time. She liked that. She insisted the desk sergeant get a message to him as soon as possible. He couldn't promise her anything.

Deciding she'd have to wait until morning to further the investigation, she readied herself for bed. Her sleeping area was cordoned off by a sliding divider. A four-poster bed, brought from her parent's home, sat in the center of the room. A small vanity and chair sat beside the window that overlooked the courtyard behind the building. A flowered love seat with a fat tabby cat curled on a cushion took up the rest of the wall space. Just as Kris was crawling beneath the down comforter, the phone rang.

"Yes?"

"Kristina, it's Gabe. I got a message you called. What's wrong?"

Kris smiled at the concern in his voice. "Nothing's wrong. But I have something to show you. Can I e-mail some pictures?"

"Can it wait until morning?"

Anxious to show him her find, she hesitated. "I suppose. It's just you said we needed proof that Frank was doing something illegal before you would question him, right?"

"Right," he replied cautiously.

"Well, I think I have the proof you need."

"Kristina, listen to me. Don't do anything or say anything about this until I get there in the morning."

Her eyebrows rose. "You want to come here?"

"Yes."

"Okay." A thrill of anticipation skipped over her skin. "First thing?"

"First thing. And, Kristina?"

"Yes?"

"Make sure you lock your doors."

"I always do," she answered before hanging up. But just to be sure, she double-checked. Sure enough, locked.

Back at her bed, she snuggled beneath the covers, convinced that tomorrow she'd be able to put Gram's mind to rest.

Hopefully, with Gabe's help.

THREE

The next morning, Gabe pulled his wool sport coat shut against the brisk air as he left his car and walked to Kristina's apartment building. He still couldn't believe she lived here.

He pushed the buzzer next to K. Worth. A moment later the door unlocked and he went inside. The large entryway was sparkling clean. The tiled floor shone with polish and the silver row of mailboxes looked brand-new. So much for slumming.

An elevator took him to the second floor. Kristina's apartment was at the far end. A large wreath sporting a red bow hung around the peep hole. He knocked on the steel door.

The door slid open. She stood there with a smile on her face. "Hi."

"Good morning," he managed to say past the tightness in his throat.

He shouldn't feel this pleased to see her. This was police business, not a social call. Yet he couldn't take his eyes off her. He really should have just had her e-mail the pictures, but he'd been curious. He wanted to know more about the woman she'd become.

Her faded jeans rode low on her hips. A bright coral, formfitting, long-sleeved sweater accentuated her curves. Her long blond hair was pulled back into a strange-looking rope with multicolored beads hanging down at the end. Mascara darkened her lashes and her lips were glossy. Inviting. His mouth went dry as memories of last night's escapade stormed through his mind. He should have kissed her and not worried about the consequences.

"Come in," she said with a sweep of her hand.

Forcing himself to focus, he stepped into her apartment and realized he'd misjudged her. He'd expected a contemporary setting with high-end furniture and expensive decorations. His gaze cataloged the interior. The walled-in, small living room looked cozy with well-worn leather seating and a scarred coffee table strewn with photography magazines. In the corner stood a small Christmas tree, the lights twinkling.

A beautifully carved, yet beat-up armoire sat against one wall. Its opened doors revealed an older television, a stereo and lots of books. To his right was a small eating area and an even smaller kitchen. And he assumed the closed, sliding partition led to her bedroom and bath.

"This way." Kristina walked toward a curtain, which she pushed aside and motioned him through.

The enormity of the loft-style photography studio surprised him. A large bay window dominated the far wall. Light stands and a stack of props took up one corner. A changing area and a workstation occupied the other two corners. The middle was open and a tripod with a camera sat at the ready.

Large photographs in minimalistic frames were stacked in a corner.

"Great space," he commented. He walked over to the framed pictures. The one face-out was of what looked like an African village.

"Thank you. It took me a while to get it the way I wanted."

"You did a good job." He motioned to the photos. "Did you take these?"

She nodded, her expression a bit apprehensive, as if his opinion mattered.

Flustered by that thought, he flipped through the stack of images. More of Africa, others looked to be in an Eastern European setting, while a few were definitely South American. All third-world communities. Impressed by both the pictures and the fact that she'd gone to these places, he said, "These are great."

"Thank you."

Her pleased smile zinged through him, creating a wave of unexpected yearning that tightened his chest. He moved away from the photos and back to business. "So, what did you have to show me?"

Her eyes gleamed with excitement. She rushed to the workstation and picked up several pictures. "Check these out."

Gabe studied the images. The first two were of Frank as he walked away from the camera toward the dark alleyway. The second showed the man in the shadows, his face unfortunately obscured by darkness. The third showed Frank handing over the envelope. The fourth was of the man emptying the contents into his hand. And the fifth was a zoomed-in shot of a dozen pills in various shapes and sizes.

Gabe raised an eyebrow. "Looks like Frank's into drug trafficking."

"See, I knew there was something off about him," she gloated, looking quite delighted with herself.

Gabe liked her enthusiasm but he couldn't let her think she'd done a good thing. The thought of her getting hurt made his shoulder muscles tighten. "Yes, you were right. But you took a risk."

The enthusiastic light faded from her blue eyes. "Didn't we have this discussion already?"

"Never hurts to reiterate. Besides, this doesn't mean he had anything to do with Carl and Lena. We still haven't established anything has happened to them."

"When will you?"

"Soon." He hoped. Then he could stop torturing himself with her company.

He moved toward the floor-to-ceiling window overlooking Christopher Columbus Park. The fountain shot water in the air and a woman with a dog jogged along the winding paved path. Beyond the park, the blue water of the Atlantic sparkled in the winter sunlight. Sails ruffled in the morning breeze. Die-hard sailors in this cold weather. He shivered.

Kristina halted beside him. "Beautiful, isn't it?"

"Very." So was she.

"On summer evenings I can watch the performance artists," she stated softly. She turned her gaze on him.

Gabe found himself staring into eyes darker than the ocean and alive with intelligence. She regarded him frankly, with no guile or coyness.

So unlike the woman she'd been.

He could like this new person. He didn't want to. He couldn't risk that kind of pain again. "I should go."

She nodded slightly, opened her mouth as if to speak but then seemed to think better of it.

"What?" he asked.

"Would you mind if I took your picture?" she asked.

A dry laughed escaped him. "I don't know…"

She moved to her camera and detached it from the tripod. "You don't have to do anything. Just be."

"Just be?" How did one "just be"?

She held the camera to her eye, the round dark lens trained on him. The soft snap of the shutter was the only sound as she moved around him. He wasn't sure if he should move or stay still, so he just stood there trying not to tense. She angled the camera and clicked away. He wondered what she saw worth photographing.

"Do you like ice cream?" she asked.

He arched an eyebrow. "Yes. Doesn't everyone?"

The click of the camera echoed in the loft. "What kind?"

"Chocolate."

She lowered the camera. "Just plain old chocolate?"

He shrugged. "Yeah."

"Okay. What are you doing tonight?"

"Tonight?" An unexpected rush of anticipation arced through him.

"I plan to take Grams for ice cream. I think she'd like to meet you. Considering."

She wanted him to hear her grandmother's story about people missing from the retirement center. "I don't think that's a good idea *considering* the last time I met your family."

She frowned. "This is my grandmother. Not my parents. I think it's important for you to meet her and see for yourself that she's not some loony person."

"I don't know." Social events with the Worthingtons weren't high on his list of repeat experiences. The last time he'd met Kristina's family, they'd made their feelings about his unsuitableness loud and clear. But this wasn't her parents, just one elderly woman. And it was his job.

"Please," she said, her blue eyes direct and earnest.

What happened to the haughty woman who'd interrupted his life yesterday? Kristina was a puzzle, one he wasn't sure he wanted to solve. But he'd gone this far, and who knew what other kinds of trouble Grams and Kristina would get in. "Okay."

She beamed. "Great. Meet us here about seven?"

"That's fine," he agreed as he walked toward the curtain.

Kristina followed him to the door. "Thank you for taking care of this," she said, indicating the pictures in his hands.

"Not a problem. Promise me you won't do any more amateur sleuthing."

She grinned. "I don't make promises I'm not sure I can keep."

He groaned. "Just stay out of trouble, okay?"

"I'll try."

Her words weren't convincing. Gabe had a feeling that trouble and Kristina would be meeting again. And he could only hope he'd be there to protect her.

Kris had picked up Sadie early in the evening and brought her back to the loft, where they waited for Gabe. She still couldn't believe she'd invited him for ice cream. And was even more surprised that he'd said yes.

Why would he say yes?

She doubted he harbored any residual feelings from their short time together that summer many years ago.

But what a summer. She'd thought she owned the world when she'd met Gabe. He had just started working for the Boston Police Department. He'd been to-die-for in his uniform. She hadn't stood a chance. Of course now she realized how foolish she'd been to think they could have a future together. He'd taken one look at her family and bolted in the other direction, leaving her heart in tatters.

She'd seen him once since then. At Meg's wedding last year. Gabe looked even more dashing in his navy pin-striped suit and tie than in his uniform. Kris had left as soon as she politely could to avoid having to talk with Gabe.

And then what did she go and do? Seek him out, hoping he'd solve the mystery of the missing residents. Brilliant. *Not.*

"Krissy, stop fidgeting," Sadie commanded from her spot on the couch as Kris continued to tidy the already neat room. "The boy will be here in due time."

With a sheepish smile, Kris refrained from straightening the magazines on the coffee table. "Sorry. I'm just anxious to find out if Gabe talked with Frank and, if so, what happened."

Sadie's gaze narrowed. "From what you told me about those pictures you took, it sounds like Frank is doing something illegal. Maybe he harmed my friends because they caught him taking their drugs."

Taking a seat beside her grandmother, Kris gathered Sadie's arthritic hands in hers. "I'm sure Gabe will figure out where your friends have gone."

"You trust this boy?" Sadie's blue eyes bored into Kris.

"Grams, he's not a boy. And please don't call him that when he gets here. And yes, I do trust him." With the mystery of the missing retirement residents. Definitely. But not with her heart. She'd tried once. Wasn't going to repeat that mistake.

Sadie grinned. "Protective of his feelings, are we?"

Kris kept her expression dispassionate. "No, of course not."

"Ah, so you just don't want to be embarrassed by your old grandmother."

Trapped, Kris shook her head. "You calling him a boy would be embarrassing. But I'm never embarrassed by you."

Sadie squeezed her hand. "At least you aren't. Your mother, on the other hand…very embarrassed."

Kris frowned, hating that her parents weren't as loving toward Sadie as she'd wished they'd be.

The doorbell rang, sending Kris's heart pounding. Taking deep breaths, she walked slowly to the door though her feet wanted to rush. But she wasn't going to let Sadie see her eagerness to see Gabe. Eagerness born out of curiosity to know what he'd found out, not because she longed to see him again. Or kiss him.

Wait a sec! Where had that thought come from? She flashed to when he'd pulled her into his embrace and shielded her from view with his body. Okay, so maybe she did want to kiss him. But only to see if kissing him as a grown-up would be different than when she was a naive girl mooning over a handsome uniformed police officer.

She tugged on the hem of her shirt and smoothed a hand down the silky fabric covering her stomach, wishing she could as easily smooth her nerves. With a smile she hoped didn't look too eager or too contrived, she opened the door.

Gabe held a bouquet of colorful flowers in his hand. Kris blinked back the sudden mist in her eyes. When was the last time a man had brought her flowers?

A very long time.

Gabe smiled but didn't offer her the flowers. "Hi."

Should she reach for them or wait until he presented them? "Hi, yourself. Come in."

She moved aside so he could enter. He slid out of his overcoat and hung it on the peg beside the door. He was so tall and good-looking in his navy slacks and red shirt stretching over his chest and flat stomach. His honey-blond hair had been tamed, revealing the slight graying at the temples. She resisted the urge to reach up and release the riot of waves.

Gabe headed straight for Sadie and, to Kris's amazement, handed her the flowers. Even as disappointment cascaded through her, her heart sighed at the sweet gesture. Sadie's face lit up with delight as she gathered the blooms close and breathed in.

"These are lovely," Sadie said, her eyes watery. "Thank you, young man."

"You're welcome," Gabe replied. His gaze sought Kris.

For a second she thought she saw a question in his eyes. Was he seeking her approval? She smiled and nodded her thanks and was gratified to see him relax. Interesting, and something to definitely think about later. But she had some other questions and wanted answers.

"So, what happened with Frank? Did you arrest him? Did he admit to selling pills? Did he do something to Carl and Lena?"

Gabe held up a hand. "Hey, there. Slow down. I did bring Frank in for questioning. He said the pills were over-the-counter stuff he was giving to a friend who couldn't afford any. He claims not to know anything about Carl or Lena. And since we haven't established anything has happened to Carl or Lena, or that the pills in the photo aren't what he claims they are, I had to release him."

Kris's shoulders dropped. "Well, what have you found out about Carl and Lena?"

"Not much. I visited the retirement center again and spoke with Ms. Faust. She's sticking to her story that both left on vacation. I saw their rooms, still full of their stuff. Ms. Faust said she'd fax over their itineraries as soon as the center's computer system came back online. Apparently they're shut down for some upgrades."

Sadie sighed, though her eyes looked troubled.

"Maybe she is telling the truth. I mean, she wouldn't risk lying to the police, would she? I'm just a senile old woman who is reading too much into things."

"But you found Carl's wallet in Frank's cart. What did he have to say about that?" Kris asked.

He shrugged. "Found while cleaning the dining hall and was going to turn the wallet over to Ms. Faust but it disappeared."

Kris hated thinking that they'd really been chasing the shadows of Sadie's imagination. But that's how it looked. And by the sympathetic look in Gabe's eyes, he thought so, too.

Needing to lighten the mood and distract Sadie, Kris said, "These are such beautiful flowers, Gabe. It was very thoughtful of you. Let me put them in a vase."

Sadie handed over the flowers with shaky hands. Kris put them in a green ceramic vase and added some water before setting them on the coffee table. "Perfect. How about we go get that ice cream?"

Gabe met her gaze, approval flashing in the warm depths. "Good idea."

"Sounds like a very good idea," Sadie agreed as she struggled to stand.

Kris and Gabe both rushed to help. As they left the apartment, Gabe supporting Sadie, he said to Kris, "Who knows, I might even try a new flavor today."

Kris arched a brow. "It will be good for you."

Once they reached the street, Gabe jogged over to his black vehicle to move it closer to the curb for Sadie.

"He's a keeper, Krissy girl," Sadie said, with a grin.

"Grams!"

Sadie gave a delicate shrug of her thin, hunched shoulders. "I'm just saying."

Heat burned Kris's cheeks. A keeper indeed.

Later that night as Kris worked in her studio printing off the latest batch of photos for a sportswear ad campaign, her phone rang. She glanced at the clock. Who'd call at this late hour?

"Hello?"

There was a brief moment of silence before Sadie spoke in a hushed, frantic voice. "Krissy, there's something strange going on here. I saw a body being wheeled into the infirmary. You have to come quick!"

Kris tried to let the words register. "Is an ambulance there?"

"No, Krissy. There's no ambulance. Would I have called you if there was?"

"I suppose not," Kris muttered.

Was this just another shadow in Sadie's mind? Sadie probably had a nightmare and was confusing her dream with reality.

But she sounded so upset.

"I'll be right there." Kris hung up, quickly dressed, then grabbed her purse and ran out the front door to the old Honda Civic parked at the curb. She started the engine and as the motor heated up, she used her cell to dial Gabe.

"Hello?"

"Hi, it's me."

"What's wrong?"

Warmed by the sudden edge in his voice, she said,

"Sadie just called me all upset. She…" What? Saw a dead body? "I'm on my way to see her."

"It's kind of late for visiting hours," Gabe commented.

"Yeah, well, Sadie needs me." She decided to be straight with him. "She thinks she saw a dead body."

"I'll meet you there. Don't do anything until I arrive."

Emotion clogged Kris's throat. "Thank you."

She hung up, glad to know that Gabe was on his way.

At this late hour, Kris saw only one other vehicle on the road as she drove to Miller's Rest. Thankfully, the van that pulled up behind her and whizzed past as she rounded the bend right before the retirement center wasn't a police car, or she'd have been ticketed for sure.

Kris didn't usually break the speed limit, but Sadie's agitation formed a ball of concern in Kris's chest. Sadie was relatively healthy, but you just never knew. Kris's heart squeezed tight.

She parked and hurried toward the front entrance. She glanced around, expecting to see the security guard patrolling the grounds.

"Psst. Over here." Sadie waved from a side entrance. She wore the thick terry robe Kris had given her for her eightieth birthday this past fall and rubber-soled bootie slippers. Her gray hair was a mess, as if she'd just rolled out of bed.

Kris hurried over. "Shouldn't this door be equipped with an alarm?"

Sadie shrugged. "It didn't go off when I opened it, so I'd say no. Come on."

"Wait. Gabe's on his way here."

Sadie's eyes widened. "Who?"

Kris's stomach clenched. She couldn't have forgotten him, could she? "Detective Burke."

"That's good thinking, Krissy girl. But I have to show you. Now."

Sadie rapidly shuffled away, leaving Kris no choice but to follow. The darkened center sent a chill creeping up Kris's spine. Dim lights along the edges of the floor illuminated the hallways.

Sadie took Kris to the infirmary. "They wheeled a body in here."

"A body?" Kris repeated, not sure she really wanted clarification.

"You know. A body under a sheet. A *dead* body."

Kris swallowed back the distaste that image brought and told herself it was just another of Gram's shadows. A nightmare she mistook for reality. Sadie pushed open the door and Kris peered over her head into the medical room. Glass-paned cabinets lined the walls, a desk with a stiff-backed chair occupied one corner. A gurney had been pushed against the far wall.

Kris sighed with relief. No body. "Well, it's gone now. And who are *they?*"

"Ms. Faust and a man."

Odd. Ms. Faust hardly seemed the type to go sneaking around at night. "Grams, you probably had a nightmare."

Sadie's chin jutted out slightly. "I couldn't sleep."

Kris raised an eyebrow. "So you went wandering."

"I—"

A door slammed. Sadie shuffled quickly to a window facing the service entrance. Reluctantly, Kris followed. A white van had backed up to the double doors off the kitchen. The rear doors of the van were open, but at this angle Kris couldn't see the contents. Ms. Faust and two men stood talking.

"Hey, that's the van that passed me on the way here," Kris whispered.

"I'll bet they put the dead body in there," Sadie said. "I wish the detective would hurry up."

"He's probably out front. Come on," Kris urged Sadie away from the window.

One of the men shut the doors before rounding the vehicle and getting in on the passenger side. The other man climbed into the driver's seat. Ms. Faust waved curtly and disappeared inside the center as the van drove away.

"We better get you out of here before she sets the alarm."

Sadie's urgent whisper galvanized Kris into panic mode. "Let's get you to your room first."

"I can take care of myself," Sadie groused. "You need to leave before we're caught." She shuffled back toward the side entrance.

With a rueful shake of her head, Kris followed. Just as Sadie reached for the handle, Kris noticed the black box on the wall next to the door. The green light hadn't been flashing when they came in. Now the light seemed as bright as a camera flash.

"Grams, no!"

Sadie pushed the door open and a loud screeching siren filled the air. Kris's warning came a second too late.

Sadie groaned. "Rats!"

"Busted," Kris said and sagged against the wall.

For the next several minutes chaos reined as the

security guard, the night nurses, Ms. Faust and several blurry-eyed residents flooded the hallway. Ms. Faust turned off the siren. The ensuing peace was welcome.

"What is the meaning of this?" Ms. Faust bellowed, looking decidedly uptight. Her gray eyes flashed behind square-framed glasses. Her brown wool dress hung on her broad shoulders. Her stiff posture revealed her distress.

Before Kris could explain, police sirens and flashing lights brought more chaos. Perfect. Gabe rushing to her aid. How embarrassing.

Her glower deepening, Ms. Faust instructed the staff to take the residents back to their rooms. With the security guard standing watch over Kris and Sadie, Ms. Faust motioned for them to follow her to the foyer.

Two cars came to a screeching halt. One a police cruiser and the other, Gabe's SUV.

Gabe stalked forward. The thunderous expression on his face let Kris know she was in deep trouble.

FOUR

"Detective Burke, whaddya doing here?" asked the older of the two officers who'd responded to the alarm.

Gabe held up his hands, palms out. "Just observing."

Kris flashed him a frown. Great, he was going to stand by and watch her humiliation. He raised an eyebrow in return.

Ms. Faust introduced herself to the officers and then turned to Kris. "Please explain what you are doing here in the middle of the night."

Sadie spoke up. "There was a—"

"Grams was having trouble sleeping and wanted some company," Kris interjected, hoping to save them from having to explain everything. She avoided making eye contact with Gabe.

Ms. Faust's hairline rose along with her dark eyebrows. "You know the rules. No guests after visiting hours."

"I apologize," Kris said in as contrite a tone as she could muster. Needing to change the subject, she took a more direct approach to the question burning in her mind. "What was that van doing here?"

Ms. Faust hesitated for a fraction of a second. "Delivering food. Now I suggest you leave, Miss Worthington, and let Sadie get her rest."

Before Kris could stop her, Sadie sidled up to the officers and explained to the two men about Carl and Lena disappearing.

Ms. Faust huffed. "I've already explained to Detective Burke—" she gestured toward Gabe, who stood off to the side "—that the residents in question have gone on vacation."

"What about the body I saw you wheel into the infirmary tonight?" Sadie pressed.

Kris cringed, wishing Grams hadn't mentioned that. But since she had… Kris watched Ms. Faust closely. A little tick started over her right eye. Was she angry, nervous or guilty?

"I have no idea what you are talking about," Ms. Faust stated.

The older officer hitched up his utility belt, glanced over at Gabe before saying, "We'll just take a look around. Won't take but a moment."

Throwing Sadie and Kris a nasty glare, Ms. Faust preceded the policemen down the hallway.

Gabe stepped forward and took Kris by the elbow. "I told you to wait for me," he said in a harsh whisper.

"I'm sorry, but Grams was so agitated. I couldn't wait," she whispered back.

He released his hold on her and ran a hand through his hair. "Are you trying to make things more difficult for Sadie?"

Guilt and concern gripped Kris by the throat. "Of course not. Help me get Grams to her room, would you?"

Gabe nodded, though his expression said he wanted to be anywhere but there. They flanked Sadie and led her to her studio.

"Grams, promise me you won't do any more wandering about at night," Kris said as she helped Sadie on the bed.

"Only if you promise to come back tomorrow."

Tucking the bedcovers over Sadie, Kris said, "I'll be here after breakfast."

"You do believe me, don't you, Krissy?" Sadie's gaze sought Gabe. "I know I didn't imagine that body."

The unreadable expression on Gabe's face didn't fool Kris. He didn't believe Sadie.

She hesitated. How did the Bible describe faith? The verse in Hebrews rushed to the forefront of her mind. *Now faith is the assurance of things hoped for, the conviction of things not seen.*

Kris stroked back a lock of Sadie's hair. Love filled her heart for this woman who'd taught her about the love of Jesus, who taught her to have faith in God. Shouldn't she put some faith in Sadie?

"I believe you, Grams." She kissed her papery-thin cheek, then she and Gabe quietly slipped out of the room.

Gabe stopped her in the hall. "You really believe her?"

"Yes, I do. If she saw a body, then she saw a body."

Gabe frowned. "You said she had a nightmare."

"She said she wasn't asleep."

"You're both nuts." He shook his head, clearly exasperated with her and Grams. Capturing her hand, he said, "Come on, let's get out of here." Gabe led the way toward the front of the center.

Ms. Faust was at the entrance door talking with the police officers.

"Ms. Faust has decided not to file trespassing charges against you, Miss Worthington," said the older officer.

Kris gave Ms. Faust a tight smile. "Thank you."

Ms. Faust inclined her head. "I realize you are devoted to your grandmother, but you must understand that at her age, it's not uncommon for the mind to become confused, mixing reality with fantasy. We may need to consider moving her to a memory care facility."

"She isn't losing her mind." Kris ignored the little niggling reminder of the few times Sadie had seemed to be more forgetful. It was one thing for Grams to lose track of a conversation but another entirely for her to make up an elaborate scenario like this. Kris turned to the officers. "My grandmother says she saw a body on a gurney. She wouldn't make that up."

The young officer's smile was slightly sad whereas the older man's was blatantly patronizing as he said, "I suggest you stick to regular visiting hours."

Kris ground her molars. The man made the center sound like some kind of prison. Under Ms. Faust's iron fist, the place certainly felt like one. Kris's gaze sought help from Gabe but his stony silence was all she received.

"It's late and I must check on the residents to see that everyone is back in their quarters," Ms. Faust announced before marching away.

With a police escort out of the building, Kris had no choice but to leave.

But she'd be back tomorrow and she would find out

what was going on in the retirement center. Her gut instinct told her it wasn't good.

Now all she had to do was convince Gabe that she and Sadie weren't crazy.

"I can't believe you did that." Gabe ran a hand through his hair in an effort to control the frustration beating along his nerve endings. "Someday your impulsiveness will hurt you."

He sat across from Kris in a diner near her loft. At this early hour they had the place pretty much to themselves except for a few other night owls. The familiar sounds of Christmas carols played in the background, the smell of bacon filled the air and the vinyl seats of the booth squeaked every time either of them moved.

"She needed me," Kris said, her big blue eyes imploring him to understand.

He understood all right. The two women were nut jobs and he'd do well to walk away right now before the insanity rubbed off on him.

Searching her face, he marveled at her loyalty. What he wouldn't give for someone to have that kind of faith in him. But that was a pipe dream for sure. Especially where Kristina was concerned. Even if she had changed since he'd cared for her, they were still worlds apart. That knowledge left a faint disquiet in his gut.

In an effort to distract himself from his thoughts, he picked up the cream container and poured a bit into his coffee.

Kris leaned forward. "Look, I know how this all

must seem, but Grams isn't losing her mind. She's as sharp as ever."

"Come on, Kristina, you have to be realistic."

She frowned. "What's that supposed to mean?"

He reached across the table and took her hand. "She's eighty years old. Maybe she's *not* as sharp as you think. You aren't with her 24/7. Maybe Ms. Faust sees more than you do."

"No." She tried to jerk her hand away but he held firm.

"I know you don't want to hear this but someone has to say it. She's—"

"She's not senile."

"Have you talked with her doctor?"

For a moment she stared at him with argument in her eyes but then she dropped her gaze and her shoulders sagged. "No, I haven't."

He hated to see her defeated but it couldn't be helped. Enabling her and Sadie in this crazy game wouldn't be good for any of them. "I think it's time you did."

She sighed. "I guess you're right." She lifted her gaze to pin him to the cushioned seat. "And if he says she's not suffering from dementia, will you take her seriously?"

"I will." He leaned closer. "And if dementia is setting in, you'll accept it?"

Her eyes narrowed slightly. "Will I have a choice?"

"You always have a choice, Kristina."

She sat back. "Really?"

"Yes, really." Knowing she'd appreciate the comparison, he said, "Isn't that what the Bible says? That God gives us free will? Choices?"

The tips of her mouth curved up slightly, though not in pleasure. "Choice is a funny thing, you know. We can choose to walk away from those who love us. We can choose to hurt those close to us. But what choice does that leave for the one left behind?"

He stilled. She wasn't talking about Sadie. She was bringing up their past. His gut clenched. "To move on. To make the most of their life without the person."

"I certainly have done that, haven't I?"

Regret for hurting her lay heavy on his shoulders. "Kris, look. What happened between us that summer was doomed to fail from the moment we met."

"What?" Fire flashed in her bright eyes. "You really believe that?"

"Yes. I told you as much then and I still believe it. We come from different worlds." And she deserved so much better than him. Someone who could fit into her world.

She shook her head. "Not that different. Not anymore. But that isn't the real reason you left me, is it?"

"Yes, it is. I couldn't be the man you wanted, needed. I saved us both a lot of unnecessary pain."

"Who said you get to decide what I want or need?" She gathered her coat and slid out of the booth to stand beside him with her gaze so full of hurt. "Just be honest. You left me because you didn't love me."

His heart constricted. Words danced in his head but refused to come out. Even as she turned and walked away, he still couldn't voice the feelings choking him.

He didn't believe in love.

But he'd cared enough about Kris to know he wasn't the right man for her. So he'd done the only honorable thing he could. He'd said goodbye. He didn't regret his decision. He'd done what was best. For her.

But that didn't mean the pain wasn't as fresh today as it had been then.

Kris stepped out into the cold night air and welcomed the stinging sensation of her tears freezing against her cheeks. What had she been thinking to bring up the past? She was over him. Or at least she'd thought she was. But having her suspicion about his feelings confirmed hurt. His silence spoke volumes; he'd denied nothing.

He hadn't loved her. He'd just used her family as an excuse to dump her.

Scrubbing at her cheeks, she sloshed through the snow toward her apartment building, half hoping Gabe would come after her.

Her mind went back to that day eight years ago when he'd broken her heart. They were supposed to have attended dinner with her parents. Kris had taken the liberty of buying Gabe a new suit because she'd ascertained the one he owned wouldn't do. Her parents already had expressed their disapproval of her relationship with a beat cop. She hadn't wanted to give them another reason to hold Gabe in disdain.

But Gabe hadn't appreciated her effort. Instead, he'd refused the suit. The dinner had been a disaster thanks to her parents' veiled barbs. When he'd taken her home, he'd told her the relationship was over because he could never fit into her world no matter how much she wanted him to change.

She hadn't meant buying him a new suit to seem that way, but he wouldn't listen.

And just like that, he had wanted her out of his life.

For months she'd held on to some hope that he'd relent and call but he never did.

Now she knew it was because he hadn't loved her. She wondered if he'd had any affection for her at all.

She should be grateful he'd broken up with her, because the breakup had been the impetus she needed to defy her parents' wishes for her life. Earning a living as a photographer hadn't been the way the Worthingtons had envisioned their daughter's future. But she'd found some happiness.

The sound of footsteps behind her echoed in the stillness and sent a shiver of apprehension skating across her skin. The darkened street held shadows of danger she hadn't noticed before. She quickened her pace and glanced over her shoulder to see the dark outline of a man following her.

She jammed her hand into her coat pocket, her fingers closing around her cell phone. Would she be able to get it out and dial 9-1-1 before the man caught up with her?

The outside door to the building was just steps away. She reaching into her other coat pocket for the keys just as a hand descended on her shoulder.

She screamed and yanked away.

"Hey, it's just me," Gabe said.

Heart beating wildly against her ribs, Kris sagged against the door with relief and pleasure. He had followed her.

The unlatched door swung open, sending her sprawling across the entryway linoleum.

"Kristina!" In a flash Gabe was there, gathering her close. "Are you okay?"

"Yeah, fine." Just a bruised ego.

Once upright, she stepped away from his concerned care. "You shouldn't sneak up on people like that."

In the dim light of the overhead fluorescent fixture, amusement played across his handsome features. "I didn't sneak up. I followed you to make sure you got home safely."

"Thank you." She tried to sound grateful but she was thoroughly irritated at him and herself for being glad to see him. Shivers started running up and down her body, making her aware of the cold swirling inside the building and of the compelling heat emanating from Gabe.

"You should talk to your neighbors about leaving that door open. It's not a safe thing to do."

"Thank you for stating the obvious," she snapped, disliking the lecturing tone in his voice.

"Whoa, sorry." He held up his hands. "Let me walk you upstairs."

Not a good idea. Not when she wanted to feel his arms wrapped around her again, warming her, protecting her. "That won't be necessary."

He nodded and stepped back. "You'll call me after you've consulted with Sadie's doctor?"

Annoyed at the reminder, she said, "Yes."

He saluted before leaving her alone at the foot of the stairs. Slowly she climbed to her floor. As she neared her front door, chills of dread ran roughshod over her shivers.

The moon's glow coming through the skylight splashed across the threatening words written in black on her door just below the wreath.

Stop asking questions. Or else.

Scrabbling with her panic, she fumbled for her phone again and scrolled the address book for Gabe's cell number. It rang.

"Pick up, pick up," she chanted, her gaze darting up and down the hall, expecting someone terrifying to come jumping out at her.

"This is Burke."

"It's me. Come back quick!"

"I'll be right there." He hung up.

Kris raced down the stairs to open the door just as Gabe came running up.

"Are you okay?"

His wild-eyed panic gave her a moment of pause. "Yes. Yes, I'm all right. Come in. You have to see this."

She led him up the stairs and pointed to her door.

He was silent for a long moment before he flipped open his cell and called the station to report a crime of vandalism.

Kris stared at the ugly words as a violent shudder racked through her body. "Something is going on at the retirement center and someone doesn't want me to find out what."

Gabe slid his arms around her. "We'll get to the bottom of this."

She relaxed into the comforting warmth he offered. "Do you believe Sadie now?"

"I'm reserving the right not to pass judgment until we have more information."

Kris sighed. She would just have to be satisfied with his paltry offer, no matter how frustrating, because she was confident Sadie was telling the truth. And Gabe would come around to that knowledge eventually. She only hoped neither she nor Sadie got hurt in the meantime.

"Did you see anyone when you came upstairs?" Gabe asked.

"No. But the front…" She shuddered. Someone had entered the building. Could they still be inside somewhere waiting to attack? "What if I'd been home when they came here?"

Gabe turned her to face him. "You're all right. I'm not going to let anyone hurt you."

She blinked back sudden tears. "You can't promise that. What if…what if the person who wrote this somehow broke into my apartment?"

She could tell from the look in his eyes that the thought had occurred to him, as well. Drawing his weapon, he took her keys and unlocked the door. Then using a handkerchief he extracted from his coat pocket, he opened the door. "Stay put," he said before disappearing inside.

Anxiousness danced in her tummy as she waited for Gabe to return.

A few moments later he came back out. "All clear."

She let out a relieved breath. "What if whoever did this comes back?"

He pulled her close to his chest with one strong arm wrapped tightly around her while his free hand rested on his holstered weapon. "Don't worry. I'll keep you safe."

She rested her cheek against the warm fabric of his

dress shirt where his overcoat hung open. His heart beat a rhythmic cadence that eased some of her tension and made her feel secure. Cocooned within his embrace, she did feel safe.

A few minutes later two uniformed officers arrived, followed closely by crime scene technicians.

Once the CSI tech was finished dusting for prints and looking for other obvious evidence, Gabe led Kris inside. "Take a look around and see if anything has been disturbed."

She did a quick walk-through of the apartment. As far as she could tell, everything was as it should be. Nothing was out of place or missing.

"That's good," Gabe said and planted her at the dinette table. "I'll be right back."

She watched him as he talked to the techs and then to the other officers. He listened carefully, then seemed to be giving instructions, in complete control of the situation. She liked that he wasn't afraid to take charge, yet he wasn't domineering with the other officers. And as he'd demonstrated earlier at the retirement center, he was comfortable letting others take the lead.

He'd changed over the years from the brash, almost cocky, young officer she'd known to this capable and confident man. A man who never loved her. And probably never would.

Restless with her thoughts and the situation, she rose to make a pot of coffee. Soon the aromatic scent of a premium French roast curled up through the steam of the coffeemaker. She poured herself a cup and set out another for Gabe. Just in case he chose to stay for a while.

Which she hoped he would, even though she knew she would only be setting herself up for more heartache if she became too attached to him again.

Finally, they were alone.

"Coffee?"

Gabe gave her a grateful smile. "Please."

"Did they find anything?"

"No." He took a seat at the table. "No prints on the door or surrounding walls. The ink used to write the message is from a permanent marker. They'd have to take the door to determine the type, but most likely it's a common brand, too difficult to trace. The front entrance door was also wiped clean. Whoever did this was careful."

"I'll order a new door tomorrow. Then they can come back and take the door." She cringed to think of her neighbors seeing the message.

"That would be good. And tomorrow I'll come back to interview the other residents, see if anyone saw someone hanging around who didn't belong."

Kris frowned. "I'm sure if anyone were loitering, the tenants would have called in a complaint."

"But someone could have slipped in, pretending to be a guest or a delivery person."

"Great. Now everyone in the building will be alarmed."

"Can't be helped."

"I know." She sipped her coffee, letting the warm liquid slide down to her empty stomach. "You do realize this is another example of God's provision, don't you?"

He peered at her from over the rim of his mug. "Your faith is admirable."

She'd take that. Maybe one day he'd find faith, too.

"Thank you for the coffee." He set his empty mug aside and took her hand. "I've got to report in. There's a uniformed officer parked right outside."

"Of course." She stood, already feeling lonely. "I'll see you in a few hours."

He gave her a crooked smile. "Yeah, a few hours. Try to rest, okay?"

"I will." She walked him to the door.

He reached out to stroke his hand down her cheek, his touch achingly tender, yet her skin felt branded by the contact.

Then he was gone. She shut the door and turned the lock, wishing that locking up her heart came with as much ease.

But with Gabe, nothing was ever easy.

FIVE

Gabe's cell phone rang, the noise cutting through the early morning quiet of the station house. He liked to get in before the chaos of another day began. He'd just arrived and hadn't even taken his coat off yet. He reached into the side pocket and pulled out his phone. "Burke."

"It's me. Sadie just called all upset. Another resident has gone missing."

Dread like a stone dropping through water landed in the pit of his stomach with a dull thud. Maybe Sadie *had* seen something last night…no, that just didn't seem plausible. "Where are you?"

"Home. But I'm heading over there right now."

"Kristina, stay put. I'll go check this out." If for no other reason than to prove to Kris nothing was going on.

"Good. That's why I called you." He could hear the smile in her tone. "But I'll see you there." She hung up.

Gabe ran a hand through his hair as frustration throbbed at his temples. The woman was too headstrong for her own good.

"Problem?"

Hanging up the phone, he answered his partner, Angie. "Maybe."

He filled her in on the situation. "I'm not sure there is anything going on but…"

"But we'll check it out." She retrieved her weapon from the lockbox before shrugging into her short woolen coat.

"I can take this alone," Gabe said, turning his car keys over in his hand.

Angie arched a dark eyebrow. "We're partners, right? We do this together. If it turns out to be nothing, no harm, no foul."

"Thanks," he offered, grateful for her easy attitude.

When they arrived at Miller's Rest in his SUV, he noted Kristina's compact car parked near the entrance. Inside, the place hummed with activity, unlike the previous night. When Gabe and Angie entered the building, the front desk receptionist buzzed the center's director. A few moments later the director came out of her office, her eyes widened behind her glasses.

"Detective Burke, what can I do for you? You did get the fax I sent, didn't you?"

"No." He made a mental note to check the station's central fax machine. "But I'll take a copy today."

Her eyebrows puckered. "Fine. If you'll excuse me I'll go pull that now."

"Later. We had a report that a resident went missing last night," he replied, watching closely for her reaction.

Her lips pursed tight for a moment. "You were wrongly informed. All of our residents are accounted for."

Relief should have poured in, but Gabe couldn't shake

the message written on Kris's door. *Stop asking questions or else.* Obviously, someone had something to hide.

"Then you won't mind if we take a look around," Angie declared, her voice making it clear the statement wasn't a request.

The director's gaze shifted from him to Angie. "Do you have a warrant?"

"Do we need one?" Angie interjected.

"Of course not." Annoyance and a flash of—was that panic?—entered her gaze. "I suppose you may 'look around' as long as you don't upset the residents. Especially after last night's episode." She glared at Gabe.

"We'll be discreet," Gabe assured her. "I'd like to speak with your medical director."

Ms. Faust turned toward the pretty brunette woman at the desk. "Sharon, would you show these officers to Dr. Crowley's office, please?"

Sharon glanced up, her dark mocha eyes regarding Ms. Faust a bit warily. "Uh, Dr. Crowley's out today. Dr. Sheffield is filling in."

"Just take them to the doctor," Ms. Faust barked.

Sharon scrambled out of her seat, catching the heel of her shoe on the edge of the desk. She righted herself, smoothing a hand down the front of her red skirt. She was taller than she appeared while sitting behind the desk. "This way."

He could feel Angie's questioning gaze as they followed Sharon down the hall.

"Last night?" Angie finally asked.

"Kristina visited her grandmother," he stated.

"And?"

"It was after visiting hours."

"I see."

He doubted that, but he didn't want to explain. Because if he did, then he'd have to examine why he'd come running when Kris called in the middle of the night.

"Gabe!"

Kristina waved at him from the doorway of an apartment.

His footsteps faltered. He hesitated, torn between his duty and the need to go to Kris.

Angie laid a hand on his arm. Her gaze flickered to Kris and back. He could read the speculation in her warm brown eyes. "Do you want me to interview the doc?"

"That would be great." He gave her a grateful smile. "Ask about the two people we know are missing and see if anyone has recently expired. And," he added as he lowered his voice, "ask about Sadie Arnold's mental health."

"You know he can't tell me anything," she countered with a frown.

"True. But I trust you to get his assessment off the record."

Again her focus flickered to Kris and back. She searched his face before heaving a sigh. "Will do."

Angie walked away, her dark ponytail swaying with each step. He hated disappointing her, but nothing was going to happen between them. Especially not with Kris in the picture. Even though he had no idea where that relationship was headed. He hurried to where Kris stood waiting.

"I'm so glad you came. Grams is all agitated," she

said in a rush, clearly agitated as well. "The director told her that Denise Jamesen went to visit her relatives in Rhode Island for the holiday. But Grams insists that Denise wouldn't do that. She's certain the body last night was Denise's."

If not for the threatening note on Kris's door, Gabe would have argued that only Sadie had seen a body, which didn't mean there had been one. But now... Something was going on. Still he wasn't sure it had to do with dead bodies. That was a little far-fetched.

He took Kris's hand. "I'll talk to Ms. Faust and find out more about Ms. Jamesen's whereabouts."

Sadie appeared next to Kris. Her wrinkled face lit up with pleasure. "Detective. So good of you to come see us."

"Ma'am," he replied. Did she remember why he was here?

"I was just telling Gabe about your friend Denise," Kris said.

Sadie's brow furrowed with concern. "She wouldn't have gone to see her nephew and his family. They didn't get along. She'd cut them out of her will years ago."

"Do you know where this nephew lives?" Gabe asked.

Sadie's pale lips puckered in thought. "Well, I can't recall."

Gabe smiled. "No worries. I'll ask Ms. Faust."

Sadie's eyes darkened. "That one's up to no good, I tell you."

Gabe exchanged a glance with Kris. Was Sadie right? Was the director up to no good? Or were they following the ramblings of a slipping mind?

The words written across Kris's door wouldn't release

their tight grip in his consciousness. Somehow the warning and Sadie's suspicions had to merge. But how?

Kris could see the questions and doubts flittering through Gabe's green eyes. On the one hand Sadie's claims could appear to be the ravings of a failing mind, but that awful threat last night on her door had been all too real.

She was just so glad he'd come to the retirement center even with his doubts. "Let us know what you find out, okay?"

Gabe touched her hand, the contact sending little tingles marching up her arm to settle near her heart. "Of course I will."

A movement in Kris's peripheral vision gave her a start, and she clutched at Gabe's sleeve.

An elegant, elderly woman appeared in the doorway of Sadie's studio apartment. "Hello, would anyone like a spot of tea?"

Okay, she was way too jumpy. She forced a smile. "Hello, Mrs. Tipple."

Evelyn Tipple's face creased into an answering smile. She had her silver hair swept back into a classic chignon. She looked coolly chic in khaki slacks with a sweater set complete with a string of pearls around her slender neck. An English rose personified. Her lively hazel eyes danced as her gaze roamed over Gabe. "Who's this handsome bloke?"

Kris suppressed a grin at the red creeping up Gabe's neck. "This is Detective Burke from the Boston P.D."

Mrs. Tipple winked at Gabe. "Oh, has someone done something wicked?"

If they only knew for sure. "We're—"

"I'm just visiting," Gabe interjected, darting a meaningful glance at Kris.

She sobered. These wonderful ladies very well might be in danger.

"I'd love some soothing tea, Evelyn, thank you," Sadie said. To Kris, she whispered, "Let me know what you find out."

With a kiss to Sadie's check, Kris answered, "Of course."

As Sadie passed Gabe, she touched his arm. His soft smile and nod made Kris's heart constrict. She loved that he was so good to her grandmother.

"I'll go talk to Ms. Faust again," he commented.

"I'll go with you."

They found her conversing with Frank, the janitor, in a small alcove at the end of the hall. Frank's eyes widened as they approached. "I ain't done nothing."

Kris wasn't surprised that Frank would think Gabe was here for him. The man made her nervous. There was something about him that was off.

"We're not here to see you," Gabe declared in a calm tone.

With a quick look at Ms. Faust, Frank scurried away, pushing his cleaning cart.

"Ms. Faust, can you tell me exactly where Denise Jamesen's relative lives?" Gabe asked, taking a notebook out of his pocket.

"Are you conducting an official investigation?" Ms. Faust inquired.

Gabe hesitated a moment before answering. "Yes."

Ms. Faust's mouth pressed into a thin disapproving line. "Then come back when you have a warrant. I'm sure if Mrs. Jamesen wished for Sadie to know where she was, she'd have left her the address herself," Ms. Faust argued with a glare directed at Kris.

"Sadie is upset and worried about her," Kris replied, trying to appeal to the woman's emotions.

Ms. Faust raised an eyebrow. "You should be more worried about your grandmother."

"Is that a threat?" Gabe asked, taking a menacing step closer.

Ms. Faust flushed. "Of course not. I only meant that Sadie has shown increasing signs of dementia. It's natural at her age." She turned her piercing gaze back on Kris. "And since you've been coming to visit her more regularly these past few months, her blood pressure has risen significantly."

The admonishment in Ms. Faust's tone strummed a chord of guilt in Kris. Were her visits too much for Sadie? Causing her too much excitement, raising her blood pressure and creating paranoia? Sadie *had* been more agitated the past few days. "Can you bring her blood pressure down?"

Ms. Faust gave her a patient look. "The doctors are doing what they can."

Implying that Kris was the source of Sadie's agitation. Kris glanced at Gabe. The tender concern and compassion filling his green eyes both pleased and irritated her. The man she'd known so many years ago wouldn't have shown such understanding, but dealing with the atrocities of police work had obviously given him an empathetic side.

And now he empathized with her.

He'd tried to tell her that maybe Sadie wasn't as healthy as she'd thought. So, okay, Sadie was eighty and Kris had probably been too enthusiastic in taking Grams out for ice cream, the theatre and dinner at Sadie's favorite restaurants. But Sadie's blood pressure didn't explain the warning slashed across Kris's apartment door.

As if reading her mind, Gabe spoke, his voice crisp and authoritative. "I'd still like the address and phone number of Denise Jamesen's relatives. And I really would suggest you cooperate rather than demanding I come back with a warrant. Makes me wonder what you're hiding."

Ms. Faust heaved a beleaguered sigh. "Follow me."

Kris slipped her arm through Gabe's. Gratefulness spread through her like a blanket against the chill of doubts Ms. Faust tried to instill. Gabe had enough of his own, Kris didn't need the other woman adding fuel to this particular fire.

"Thank you," she whispered.

He covered her hand, warmth seeping in and curling up her arm.

His voice dropped in volume. "Let's concede the fact that Sadie's imagination may be running rampant."

Indignation roared like a hungry bear through Kris. She didn't want to concede anything. Acknowledging Sadie's deteriorating health would be too upsetting. She tried to withdraw her hand. He wouldn't release her.

"And," he continued, his voice low, his gaze intense, "someone feels threatened enough by her ramblings to send you a warning to back off. So in one way or another, she's hit a nerve. We just have to find out with who and why."

Though her indignation lessened, Kris eyed Gabe with suspicion. "How do we find out?"

"Follow the leads we have for now."

They stopped at Ms. Faust's office door. She gave no invitation to enter so they stood in the doorway while she rummaged through papers and files on her desk. She settled on a manila file with a green tab. Flipping the cover back, she quickly wrote out the re-quested info on a hot-pink sticky note and offered the slip of paper to Gabe. "I hope this will put an end to this nonsense."

"And I'll take the itinerary," Gabe said.

With her mouth clamped tight in obvious irritation, she picked up a sheet of paper and handed it to him.

A quick scan of the itinerary revealed nothing Ms. Faust hadn't already stated. "This doesn't mention the name of the cruise ship or the return date for Carl."

She shrugged. "That's all I have."

Which was of no help.

Gabe inclined his head. "We appreciate your coop-eration."

"Yes," Kris added. "Thank you."

The woman harrumphed before indicating she'd like to shut the door.

Kris read over Gabe's shoulder as he took out his cell phone and dialed the number on the paper. He clicked his phone shut. "Busy."

Kris frowned. "Who doesn't have call waiting now-adays?"

He shrugged. "Apparently these people." He looked at the square sheet in his hand. "Tim and Edna Jamesen."

"Try again," Kris said, anxious to find out one way or another if Denise Jamesen had gone to visit her relatives for the holiday.

A second attempt yielded the same result.

"I'll call the local law enforcement and see if they can stop by the Jamesen house."

"But that could take hours or days." Sadie would be upset until she knew for sure. "It's, what, an hour and a half drive to Rhode Island?" She checked her watch. "I think I'll go check on Denise myself. I could be there by one and back by five."

"No. I'm not going to let you go off by yourself on some road trip."

Kris smiled sweetly. "Then you're volunteering to come with me. How wonderful. My car or yours?"

Gabe blinked. He shook his head as if trying to make sense of what just happened. "I didn't say I was going with you."

"But you just said you wouldn't let me go alone."

His jawline hardened. "You're not going, period."

Drawing closer, she stared up into his handsome face. "Let's get one thing straight. I don't take orders from you. I'm going to Rhode Island with or without you. Your choice."

Dark clouds gathered in his expression. Kris almost backed down. Almost. But she liked thunderstorms and he didn't scare her.

Finally, he blew out an exasperated breath. "Fine. I need to touch base with my partner. We'll take your car."

Elated with his decision, Kris put her hand on his chest, over his heart. She could feel the thud against her palm through his dress shirt and suit jacket. "Thank you."

His mouth twisted in a wry smile. "You'll be the death of me, Kristina Worthington."

Her eyes widened in horror. "Let's hope not."

He took her hand and pressed a kiss to her palm. "No worries." He released her hand. "I'll go find Angie, you say goodbye to your grandmother. Meet me in the parking lot."

Kris stared after him as he headed down the hall. The spot on her hand tingled where his lips had caressed the skin.

With a smile, she went in search of Sadie. Then it hit her. He'd given her an order.

And she was gladly obeying.

Maybe he had more power over her than she was comfortable with. What a disturbing thought.

Kris found her grandmother in the common room, an airy space with comfortable-looking sofas, a television, a coffee bar and several tables strategically placed. Near the floor-to-ceiling window overlooking the court- yard, two elderly men sat playing a game of chess. Several residents watched the news, which had the local weatherman predicting more snow in the greater Boston area.

Near the lovely stone fireplace, a large Christmas tree twinkled with red and gold decorations. From a table set off to the side, yet in a place to receive the warmth of the fire, sat Sadie, Mrs. Tipple and two other women. A silver tea service dominated the white linen tablecloth. The women sipped from delicate, floral-patterned tea cups.

Kris approached the table, glad to see her grandmother's smile as the women chatted. She didn't look stressed or jittery. Kris put her hand on her grandmother's shoulder to draw her attention. "Grams."

Sadie blinked up at Kris. "Krissy, dear, what a nice surprise. I didn't know you were coming today. Let me introduce you to my friends."

Kris's heart thudded and her stomach dropped. Her grandmother hadn't remembered she was here. Not good, not good at all. She forced a smile of greeting. "Ladies, do you mind if I steal my grandmother away for a moment?"

"By all means," Vivian Kirk, the woman sitting across from Sadie, said. She didn't look nearly as old as the other ladies. She was a plump motherly type with cool gray eyes, apple cheeks and short, blond hair. A colorful afghan was draped over her wide shoulders.

Kris helped Sadie to her feet and led her to a quiet corner in the room. "Uh, Grams, we were just in your apartment a little bit ago. Don't you remember?"

Confusion entered Sadie's eyes. "Well, now that you mention it."

"You called me about Denise Jamesen," Kris prompted, hating the distressing idea that Sadie's mind was in fact fading.

The blank look on Sadie's face nearly brought tears to Kris's eyes. Grams didn't remember.

Then Sadie's expression cleared and her eyes widened. "Oh. Oh, my. Denise is missing. Just like…just like…" She frowned, her face a study in concentration.

"Carl and Lena?"

"Yes!" Sadie grabbed Kris's hand. "What'll we do? We have to find them. Something bad has happened."

Relief made Kris's head throb. Just a momentary lapse of memory, nothing more. "We'll find them. Gabe and I are going to drive to Rhode Island to see Denise."

"You are? Wonderful. May I come?"

The eagerness in her expression plucked at Kris. "It's a bit of a drive."

"You don't want me to come?" Hurt filled her voice.

"That's not it at all," Kris quickly assured her. "I don't want to tire you out."

"Nonsense, let me just get my coat." Sadie shuffled away toward her studio apartment.

"Is everything all right, my dear?" Mrs. Tipple asked as she came to stand on Kris's right.

"Did I hear Sadie say she was getting her coat? Are you taking her away?" Vivian's concerned voice shook slightly as she moved to stand on Kris's left.

Kris gave each woman a reassuring smile. "We're just going out for a drive. We'll be back this afternoon."

Mrs. Tipple laid her hand on Kris's arm. "It's just beautiful the way you dote on your grandmother."

"Thank you." Maybe these women would know something useful. "Do either of you remember Denise Jamesen mentioning she was going to visit her relatives for the holiday?"

The two women exchanged a glance.

"She mentioned family, but I was under the impression they were estranged," Mrs. Tipple said.

Vivian nodded. "That's true, but it *is* Christmas. She

may have decided it was time to mend some fences. It's so sad to be alone at this time of the year."

"Too true," Mrs. Tipple agreed. "At our age, one doesn't want to leave this world with unfinished business."

Mrs. Tipple's words resonated through Kris. That sounded reasonable. "Is Denise ill?"

"No," Mrs. Tipple said then frowned. "At least I don't remember her being ill. Though there has been a touch of the flu going around."

"Flu season." Vivian shrugged. "You'd have to ask the doc or Ms. Faust."

She doubted Ms. Faust would be receptive to any more questions. "Thank you, ladies. I should make sure Grams doesn't need help with her coat."

Kris found Sadie standing in the middle of the room, coat in hand, a bemused expression on her face. She stared at Kris. "I have my coat. Are we going somewhere? I do so love to have adventures."

Kris's heart dropped. Had she forgotten already? "We're driving to Rhode Island to see Denise."

Sadie frowned. "She's not there. Why would she go there?"

"That's what we'll find out," Kris said.

Sadie brightened. "All right then. Let's go, Krissy, we don't have all day. It's a long ride."

Sadie shuffled toward the door.

"Uh, Grams, shouldn't you put on some shoes?"

Sadie blinked and looked down at her fuzzy slippered feet. "Oh, my, yes. These won't do all at."

Hating to see her grandmother so befuddled, Kris helped her change into a pair of sturdy-soled, leather shoes.

At the front desk, Kris signed Sadie out of the center without any fuss. Outside, the frigid December air turned their breaths to puffs of smoke as they made their way across the parking lot to the compact car Sadie had given to Kris when it had become clear Sadie could no longer drive.

Kris halted with a gasp.

"Krissy?"

Her mouth had gone dry, preventing any words from escaping. Fear and outrage vied for prominence in her thoughts.

Someone had slashed all four tires.

SIX

Kris scanned the parking lot and saw no one amid the few cars. Whoever had done this was long gone, and as far as she could tell, only her car had been vandalized.

A deep sense of violation embedded itself inside Kris, right next to a big heap of fear. Someone had known her plans. How? She shuddered with growing horror.

She had to tell Gabe.

Taking Sadie by the arm, she propelled her back toward the center.

"We aren't going?" Sadie asked.

"Not today. I just realized I have a flat tire." Four to be exact.

Kris reached for the center doors just as Gabe opened the door. His surprised gaze slid to Sadie and then Kris. "What's up?"

"We can't go find my friend today," Sadie said.

Kris stomach tumbled at the forlorn look on Sadie's face. She wrapped an arm around Sadie's shoulder. "We'll go another time, Grams. Let's get you inside where it's warm."

He raised his eyebrows as he opened the door for them.

"I'll explain later." She squeezed his arm as she passed him. "Go check out my car."

His gaze sharpened, darkened with concern. "You okay?"

Touched that his first question was of her well-being, she welcomed the curl of warmth wrapping around her, smothering her distress. "With you here, I am."

The second the words left her mouth, she realized how revealing they were and another sort of fear engulfed her.

He blinked, barely concealing the pleased surprise in his mesmerizing eyes. He gave a curt nod. "Good to know."

He left to see the damage done to her car, while Kris wondered at the damage she was allowing to her heart.

"Thanks, Angie," Gabe said before following Kris out of the police sedan.

Angie had driven them to the station and stopped next to his vehicle. She now regarded him with a mixture of concern and wariness. "Are you sure about this?"

Gabe glanced over his shoulder at Kris waiting patiently by the passenger door. She was so pretty with the winter sun touching her hair like a cool kiss. He fought for detachment, but found little. He'd do whatever necessary to protect her. He turned back to Angie. "Yes, I'm sure."

"Okay, then. I'll let you know if we find anything useful on the car."

"Thanks, you're the best."

She stared straight ahead. "Right. You know the vandalism might not have anything to do with the retirement center." She slid her dark-eyed gaze back to him. "Are you sure your friend isn't mixed up in something else?"

"The thought has crossed my mind." Kris took pictures for a living. What if she'd captured something on film that someone didn't want revealed? Or was there something more sinister? He'd have to find out.

"Be careful."

"Always."

As soon as the door clicked shut, Angie drove away.

Clearly, she didn't approve of his decision to go with Kris. Couldn't be helped. If the vandalism was related to the center, then obviously someone didn't want the missing woman found. But if there was something else going on, the best way for him to uncover the truth was by sticking close to Kris.

"Ready?" he asked as he opened the passenger door for Kris.

Squaring her shoulders, she nodded and got into the car. "Definitely."

"Good." He closed the door. He admired her determination and commitment, regardless that her impulsiveness concerned him. The woman she'd become also had spunk and a level head, traits he liked in a female. But he reminded himself of his partner's warning. What else might Kris be mixed up in? Had she been telling him the truth?

As he drove them out of the city, he asked Kris more in-depth questions about her life and job.

"Why do I get the feeling I'm being interrogated?" she inquired.

Keeping his gaze on the road ahead, he replied, "I'm

curious. I want to know more about you and what you've been doing the past eight years."

"I might buy that if we hadn't already covered the timeline of my life already. And now you're questioning me about my clients?"

He decided to level with her. "I'm trying to ascertain if the vandalism could be related to your work or something else you're involved in, rather than Sadie and her sightings."

She huffed. "It's not. Most of my work is commercial assignments for reputable companies. I take pictures for their ads. I don't get involved in their affairs."

"But maybe during a shoot you photographed something you shouldn't?"

"I don't see how, considering I do most of my work in my studio. You're grasping for some explanation that doesn't exist. Someone defaced my apartment door and slashed my tires because someone doesn't want whatever is going on at the center to be uncovered."

"What about your personal pictures? All the beautiful photos in your studio?"

Her eyebrows drew together. "All those pictures were taken months ago. And if all of this had to do with my work, then why the message about not asking questions? Doesn't make sense."

She had a point. "Tell me…why do you go by Kris Worth instead of your real name?"

"You wouldn't understand."

"Try me."

She seemed to consider her words for a moment. Then said, "I wanted autonomy from the Worthington name."

Taken aback by that revelation, he said. "Autonomy? Why? Wouldn't using your family's name open more doors?"

She turned to fully face him. Her expression so becomingly earnest. "That's just it. I didn't want doors opened because of my being born a Worthington. I want doors to open because of my work."

He'd have thought she would want to capitalize on her family's clout. The woman he'd known would have taken advantage of any open doors but apparently this new Kris, full of intrigue and honor, didn't. He admired that about her. "How do your parents feel about that?"

She shrugged and straightened. "They don't like it."

The tone of her voice conveyed the conflict that he guessed raged between her and her parents. "I can imagine. It must be hard to know their daughter doesn't want to be associated with them."

"You make it sound like I've completely shut them out of my life," she said, her voice full of hurt.

He gentled his tone. "I remember a time when their approval meant the world to you."

She closed her eyes for a moment. When she opened them and met his gaze, there was such determination in those blue depths. "Not anymore. I realized that my need for their approval was also their way of controlling me."

"That's very enlightened of you."

One corner of her mouth rose in a self-effacing smile. "Years of therapy."

He sucked in a breath as concern arched through him. Was she the one with the mental issues, not Sadie? He dismissed that thought quickly. Seeing a counselor was a very common practice nowadays. And it was healthier for her to talk through her problems with a trained professional than…what he did. He buried himself in his job so he didn't have to deal with his issues. That was a disturbing thought. One he really didn't want to examine too closely. "Are you still seeing your therapist?"

She shook her head. "No. Not since I returned from Europe three months ago. I prayed a lot about it and didn't feel God leading me to continue."

"God talks to you?" That did sound a bit on the edge of reason.

She chuckled softly. "Yes. Not in an audible voice. It's more of an inner knowledge." She made a face. "It's hard to explain."

His doubts about God rose sharply. "I'll bet."

She narrowed her gaze. "You said you've experienced gut feelings."

He knew where she was going with this. "Yes. I know you think that they were God protecting me."

She nodded. "I do. Why is that so hard for you to believe?"

He didn't have an answer. There was nothing concrete to prove or disprove her claim. And that bugged him. He liked absolutes even though life was unpredictable.

A thick silence stretched between them.

She shifted on the seat. "You know, it occurs to me we never talk about you or your family. Why is that?"

A knot formed in his stomach. "Nothing to say."

"How's your mother?"

"Good."

"Did she ever marry the doctor?"

Surprise flickered deep inside. She'd remembered while he hadn't thought about that in years. "I'd forgotten about him. No, that fizzled out like all of her relationships."

"Does she have many?"

He gave a tight laugh as old hurts resurfaced. "Yes. Mom's always on the quest for true love." He scoffed. "Like it exists."

She let out a tiny gasp. "You've never been in love?"

He briefly met her gaze. Kris sucked in air as she stared at the pain there. Obviously he'd loved someone once. Not her, though. Her, he'd walked away from and never looked back. She hated that that ancient wound still throbbed.

A loud bang startled her. The SUV shuddered and fishtailed as a tire blew.

Gabe yelled, "Get down." With one hand he pushed her toward the floorboard.

A second later a deafening noise reverberated within the vehicle and the passenger window exploded inward. Kris screamed as a shower of glass rained down on her, stinging her exposed flesh. They hadn't accidently blown a tire as she'd first thought.

Someone was shooting at them. Panic rioted within her, constricting her breathing. Surreal horror clouded her vision.

The squealing of the tires and the sickening, out-of-control movements of the vehicle on the slick, snowy road sent more waves of terror down her spine and words burst from her mouth. "Please, Jesus, save us."

Gabe's expression was granite hard as he tried to maintain control of the vehicle.

But it was the blood seeping through his coat jacket on the top of his shoulder that sent her breathing into panic mode.

He'd been shot!

Please, God, don't let him die.

With adrenaline pumping through his body, Gabe brought the SUV to a limping halt alongside the shoulder of the highway. He'd driven as far as the vehicle could go; now they were sitting ducks if their shooter chose to come after them.

Keeping his head low and his eyes alert, he turned off the engine. He withdrew his weapon from his holster with one hand while he dialed 9-1-1 on his cell with the other. For a flash of a second he considered handing the phone to Kris, but she was so tightly balled up on the floor, he didn't want to take precious moments while she got herself together enough to make the emergency call.

In a voice remarkably calm considering how tight his throat muscles felt, he explained the situation to the operator and hung up with the assurance that backup was on its way.

"Gabe?"

His heart squeezed with fear. Realizing how close Kris had come to being plugged full of lead made a ripple of terror run through him, chased quickly by rage. She could have been killed. "You okay?"

"I think so." Glass glittered in her blond hair like little diamonds. She started to rise from her crouched position on the floor.

Putting his hand out to stop her, he said, "Stay down."

She stilled and frowned at him. "But you're hurt."

He glanced at his shoulder, the stinging pain just barely registering. Blood seeped through the gaping hole in his suit jacket, staining the navy material a darker crimson. Droplets of his blood were splattered on the window. The slug was embedded in the door frame. "Just a grazing. Superficial."

He flung open the door. Kris's big blue eyes stared at him with questions and concern. "I need to assess the damage to the car," he explained.

With his senses on high alert, he cautiously climbed out. Disregarding the pain radiating down his arm, he held his gun in a two-handed grip, pointed down and at the ready. Putting the vehicle between him and the few cars that zoomed past, his gaze raked over the snowy countryside along the stretch of highway. The bare trees provided little hiding space for a sniper now.

Where had the shooter been hiding?

He remembered they'd passed a service road a few miles back. The shooter had obviously driven down the road until out of view and walked to the tree line where he had taken his shots.

Anger for not having had the foresight to think of an ambush made Gabe's blood pressure rise. He let loose with a vicious kick to the shredded remains of the front tire.

Kris sat up. "What was that?"

"Nothing." His foot throbbed as his fury simmered his blood.

The whir of sirens approaching at a fast clip filled the air. Within minutes two French blue Massachusetts state cruisers with their distinctive electric-blue striping flanked the disabled SUV. Four state troopers emerged from the vehicles, their flat-brimmed navy hats pulled low over their ears and the collars of their dark blue jackets turned up against the cold. The troopers fanned out, black boots crunching over the packed snow.

A white-and-blue-striped ambulance arrived within seconds. The EMTs jumped out and rushed over to Gabe and Kris.

"I'm not hurt," Kris declared to the paramedic who was trying to take her blood pressure. "Take care of him."

"We are, ma'am," the man replied.

After a paramedic tended to his wound by cleaning and bandaging his shoulder and putting his arm in a sling, Gabe explained the situation to the officer in charge.

"So you had a civilian with you while investigating the disappearance of a woman from a retirement center?"

Gabe flinched at the censure in Trooper Davidson's tone. A tall man with deep-set eyes and a full mustache, he had a no-nonsense demeanor that inspired confidence and undoubtedly instilled intimidation in most folks.

"I didn't expect trouble. I figured we'd find the lady safe with her relatives and Kris, uh, Miss Worthington, could stop worrying."

"Well, sounds to me like someone doesn't want you all to find the lady."

Gabe's shoulder burned. "Looks like."

"I'll take you and Miss Worthington back to Boston," said Davidson. "I've sent a car down that service road you mentioned. They'll search the area, hopefully find some casings, and if we're lucky, maybe something to nail the creep who did this."

"How far are we from Woonsocket?"

"Ten, fifteen miles."

Frustration pounded at Gabe's temple. "Would you take us to Woonsocket first? Someone went to an awful lot of trouble to keep us from our destination. I really wouldn't want them to win."

Davidson contemplated him for a moment. "Not my jurisdiction."

"You would just be transport. Nothing official."

He seemed to consider before answering. "I s'pose we could take a detour. What happens if the lady in question is there?"

Gabe shrugged and winced at the pain radiating from the wound on his shoulder. "We verify that she's safe. Nothing else."

"And if she's not?"

"Then I have a lot of work to do."

"All right." He turned toward his men. "Gonzales, Smith, stay here with the vehicle until the tow truck arrives to take it to the crime lab."

Davidson gestured toward his cruiser, where Kris sat waiting. "Let's go."

Gabe slid onto the front seat then looked at Kris. "You sure you're not hurt?"

"Yes. Just a few superficial cuts from the glass. You?" She gestured to his shoulder.

"Can barely feel it. Davidson agreed to take us to the Jamesens before returning us to Boston. You okay with that?"

"Of course," she stated, her gaze determined. "We can't let the bad guys win."

Gabe grinned, liking her spirit. "No, we can't."

"That was close, though, you know." A pensive look overtook her sweet face. "One of us could easily be dead right now."

"But neither of us are."

"By the grace of God." Tears welled in her eyes.

Gabe abandoned the front seat and moved to sit beside her in the back. He gathered her close and marveled how right, how natural it felt to have her in his embrace. "You've been through a lot. I'll have Davidson just take us home."

She pulled away and wiped at her tears. "No. We have to find out if Denise is safe. Because if she isn't, then neither is Sadie."

"Then that's what we'll do."

"Thank you."

He lost himself in her beautiful eyes so full of trust and another emotion he could barely believe…affection. A matching emotion churned in his heart, wanting to escape. He tried to hold it back, tried to deny that his feelings for her were anything more than general concern.

But deep inside he knew he was only lying to himself.

Knowing they made a frightful pair with Gabe's arm in a sling and her hair tousled after attempts to extract the tiny shards of glass, Kris hoped the Jamesens would agree to talk with them. She followed Gabe up the walkway to the small cottage. Obviously upkeep on the place wasn't a high priority for the Jamesens if the chipped paint and the dark mold stains growing along the bottom edge were any indication.

The porch creaked beneath their feet. Gabe rapped his knuckles hard on the front door. The blare of a television receded and heavy footsteps approached the door.

Gabe reached toward Kris. "More glass," he murmured as he plucked at the strands.

The door was yanked open by a rather large woman in her fifties. "What do you want?"

Kris involuntarily stepped back as Gabe stepped forward, blocking the doorway and flashing his badge. "Detective Burke, Boston P.D. We have some questions. Are you Mrs. Jamesen? Edna Jamesen?"

"Yeah," she replied in a wary tone.

"May we come in?" Gabe asked.

Her suspicious gaze roamed over Gabe then darted between them before going over Kris's shoulder to where Davidson waited in his marked cruiser. "Yeah. Fine."

Once inside, nausea threatened to turn Kris's stomach. The house reeked of cigarette smoke and some unidentifiable odor Kris hoped wasn't food. Something that smelled that bad couldn't be healthy.

"We're looking for Denise Jamesen. Is she here?" Gabe inquired, his voice stern.

"No, she's not here and wouldn't be welcome," Edna Jamesen indicated in a raspy voice, hands on her ample hips. Her light brown eyes were yellowed at the edges and bloodshot as she stared down at Kris and Gabe.

Taken aback by the woman's hostility, Kris stared at the bleached blonde, wondering how anyone could be so cold.

"Have you heard from her recently?" Gabe continued.

Tim Jamesen answered from his place in an overstuffed recliner. "Naw, I haven't spoken to my aunt since my brother Tommy died of an overdose twenty years ago." He was a big man, with a burly chest, thick arms and legs. His receding hairline exaggerated the size of his forehead.

"Did you and your aunt have a fight?" Gabe guessed as he jotted on his notepad.

"You could say that. She'd wanted to get my twin, Tommy, into rehab but he wouldn't go. She thought I should have made him. Like I'm his keeper or something. He was never anything but trouble," Tim said. "But he was auntie's favorite. When he died, she cut me out of her will altogether. Not that I think the old bat has much to leave anyone, what with that fancy place she lives in."

"You've checked up on her?" Gabe pointed out.

"Not Tim, me," Edna clarified. "I tried to see her a few years ago. Wanted to make her change her mind about cutting us out." She crossed her arms over her chest. "She said we weren't family anymore."

Tim hoisted himself out of his chair. "Why you asking all these questions?"

"She's missing. Someone at the retirement center suggested she'd come to visit you," Kris informed. But obviously Ms. Faust was wrong. Or had lied.

That one's up to no good, Sadie had said. Was it true?

"Well, I'm sure she'll turn up. Bad pennies always do," Edna remarked.

"Thank you for your time," Gabe said as he steered Kris back to the car.

Davidson opened the vehicle's back door as they approached. Gabe went around to the front this time, leaving Kris in the backseat alone. She missed having him so close. She settled against the seat and stared at the houses going by as they left the rural neighborhood.

"That was horrible," she observed. "Those people were so callous. Just because they'd had a spat with Denise doesn't mean they shouldn't care what happens to her."

Davidson glanced in the rearview mirror. "I take it she wasn't there."

"No, she wasn't," Gabe confirmed.

Kris wrapped her arms around her as the cold seeped in. "It's just so sad that one's family could be so very distant and have such anger between them."

Gabe glanced over his shoulder with a raised eyebrow. "Family issues can get complicated."

Somehow she had the feeling he wasn't just referring to the Jamesens. "Yes, they can." Hers certainly had. Her parents wanted her to be one way while she fought to be another. A subject that kept a wall between them.

Gabe faced forward and lapsed into a silence that deepened with the passing miles. Just as they neared the city limits, the distinctive music of Beethoven's Fifth filled the car and jolted Kris's nerves. She scrambled to dig out her cell phone from the bottom of her purse. Moving aside the powder compact and lipstick, her wallet and a tin of breath mints, she finally grabbed her compact flip phone. She checked the caller ID. Her mother. What timing.

"Hello, Mom."

"Kristina, you have to come home now," her mother said, her voice full of anxiety.

Panic slammed into Kris. "Mom, what's wrong?"

"It's—"

The phone made a dinging noise that indicated the call was dropped. She tightened her hand around the phone. She tried calling back but the message "call failed" kept playing across the screen.

"Kris?" Gabe asked.

Numbly, she lifted her gaze to meet his. "Something's wrong at my parents'. I can't get through. The call keeps failing."

"Did she say what?" He handed her his cell phone.

"No." A terror-inducing thought struck Kris as she dialed her parents' number. "You don't think that whoever shot at us went after my family, do you?"

A look passed between Gabe and Davidson. Davidson used the car radio to dispatch a unit to the Worthington address.

Clearly they thought it was a possibility. Kris's stomach knotted and fear lodged in her throat. With frustration she hit the end button. "Now it's busy."

Davidson hit the siren and pressed on the gas pedal. The car shot forward. As the world outside whizzed by in a blur, Kris sent up a silent prayer of protection for her parents.

What had she dragged her family into?

SEVEN

The white-and-blue-striped Boston Police Department's cruiser's flashing lights announced their presence as Davidson brought the car to a halt twenty minutes later. Glad to see the call for backup was answered in such a timely fashion, Gabe helped Kris out of the car.

He put a restraining hand on her arm as she tried to rush toward the red brick, multi-leveled home in the middle of the block. "Let me check out the situation."

The sight of tears gathering in her eyes knocked around his chest, making him ache to pull her close. He settled for giving her arm a reassuring squeeze.

"Hurry, please," she whispered.

"I'll stay with her," Davidson stated as he came around the front of his car.

Grateful to the trooper, Gabe nodded and hurried toward the front door. He flashed his badge for the officer standing guard before entering. Muted, angry voices assaulted him as he stepped inside.

He focused on a gold gilt mirror that dominated one wall of the entryway and reflected the opposite room where Mr. and Mrs. Worthington were loudly arguing with two officers.

The Worthingtons appeared unharmed.

Light coming through the arched windows revealed the multitude of books shelved on the floor-to-ceiling, built-in cases. A massive desk with a leather captain's chair dominated the center of the room. Charles Worthington and his wife, Meredith, stood facing the door, making it clear they were angry at the official intrusion.

Relieved that, for the moment at least, there was no immediate threat, Gabe paused. The house was just as he remembered it. Just as stunning, overwhelming and way out of his league. High ceilings, marble floors, a gleaming wood banister and intricate crown molding on warm, beige walls. He didn't belong in this place. He'd known that the first time Kris had insisted on bringing him here.

A seriously miserable ordeal for him. Not only had he regretted not wearing the suit Kris had bought, but he'd surmised that even with the suit, he'd have been sorely out of place. Drinking from crystal glasses and eating off gold-trimmed china wasn't something he'd experienced before. His nerves had been shot by the time the evening ended and he had made the decision that he and Kristina Worthington weren't a match.

No matter how much he'd wished they were.

With a little jolt, he realized he still harbored the illogical yearning.

With a shake of his head to clear his thoughts, Gabe slipped into the study. "Officers, may I?"

The patrolmen turned in unison. After a quick scan of his badge, the officers nodded and took their leave.

"What is the meaning of this?" Mr. Worthington demanded. He wore wool slacks and a thick cable-knit sweater which made his salt-and-pepper hair and light blue eyes stand out. His tanned complexion suggested time spent outside someplace other than Boston in the winter. He narrowed his gaze. "Don't I know you?"

Surprised, Gabe gave a short nod. That Mr. Worthington recognized him after all these years and after only having met once was impressive. "I'm Detective Burke. Your daughter Kris is a friend. She was very worried when she received what to her sounded like a panicked call from Mrs. Worthington."

"Burke? Gabriel Burke?" Mrs. Worthington peered at him for a moment. She was a stunning woman with honey-blond hair, her figure trim in navy trousers and a red fuzzy sweater set. And a complexion as equally tanned as her husband. "What happened to your arm?"

"A superficial wound." He braced himself as she inspected him.

Obviously she, too, remembered the unacceptable man her daughter had once brought home. And clearly, judging by the slight curl to her lips, she still didn't find him acceptable.

"Where is my daughter?" Mrs. Worthington asked, her tone suspicious.

"Outside. Why did you call?" he questioned, still unsettled by the shooting.

"What business is it of yours? Did you send those officers barging in?" she inquired.

"Your daughter was concerned. She couldn't reach you after your call. She asked for help."

Mr. Worthington gestured toward Gabe's arm. "That happen in the line of duty?"

Gabe inclined his head. "Yes, sir."

A flash of respect in the older man's eyes unnerved Gabe. "I'll let Kris know it's safe to enter," he said and made a hasty exit, glad to be away from the disquieting stares.

He stepped outside, took a deep breath of cool air and motioned to Kris. She rushed over.

Her blue eyes searched his face. "Are they all right?"

He nodded. "Yes. I don't think the call had anything to do with…"

She held up a hand and let out a relieved breath. "Good." She started forward then stopped; her big blue eyes stared at him with anxiety. "Do I look okay? Not too disheveled? We can't tell them. They'd only be upset."

"Let's just find out why your mother called," he suggested, not willing to promise her that he wouldn't tell her parents of the danger threatening their daughter. "And you look beautiful as always."

A tinge of pink touched her cheeks as she made a face before going inside to her parents.

Gabe thanked Davidson before the trooper took off. Gabe then called Angie, filled her in and gave her the Worthingtons' address so she could pick him up. He hoped to convince Kris to stay here where she'd be safe.

He found the Worthingtons had moved into the living room, an airy space with more windows showing off a large patio filled with bare bushes and covered furniture now dusted white with snow. Comfy couches and armchairs in muted pastel patterns were placed strategically before a large open fireplace. Flames danced from the gas fire, emitting a pleasing warmth. Kris had taken off her coat and was sitting beside her mother on the couch. Mr. Worthington stood off to the side, a perturbed expression on his face.

Feeling like an intruder, Gabe cleared his throat to get Kris's attention.

All three Worthingtons stared at him. The heat in the room seemed to rise. He resisted the urge to loosen his tie.

"The 'emergency' Mother called about was a fundraiser that she wants me to attend next Saturday," Kris stated, suppressed anger echoing in every word. "A whole week and a half away."

"Ah." He was glad it wasn't anything serious…but a fundraiser had required a panicked call?

"It's very important we fill our table. The Corringtons canceled. It's so like them. Why we stay friends with them is beyond me. Very last minute. Quite rude," Mrs. Worthington elaborated. "I'll really need to let the organizers know the guest list. I expect you there, but you'll need to bring a date." She glanced toward Gabe, her gaze assessing.

Kris shot him an apologetic look before addressing her mother again. "You'll have to find someone else to fill your table. I'm not interested in going."

"Surely you're not doing anything you can't get out of. We have a family obligation to fill this table," Mrs. Worthington insisted, her voice rising slightly.

Shaking her head, Kris stared at Gabe with a "see what I have to put up with" expression. He felt for her. Clearly she didn't want to join her parents. Her mother was being overbearing. He remembered Kris's comment about wanting autonomy. Now he understood.

Seeing the beseeching look on Kris's face, Gabe heard himself say, "Actually, Kris and I already have plans for next Saturday."

What? Okay, that came out of left field. Dating her wasn't on his agenda, but he couldn't stand to see her railroaded into appearing at a function she obviously didn't want to attend. He felt as protective of her now as he did when bullets were slamming into the car.

He'd take her to a basketball game or…the ballet. She used to like that. Some place social, public. Where there was no chance of letting the situation become emotional.

The small, surprised smile on Kris's face made his stomach do a funny little flip. He lifted his uninjured shoulder in a half shrug to convey he was as surprised by his words as she was.

"Then change your plans. You'll both join us. You will have to wear a tux. These affairs are formal," Mrs. Worthington instructed as if the matter were settled.

He choked and covered it with a quick cough.

Kris jumped to her feet. "Mother! No. I don't want to attend your function."

Mr. Worthington cleared his throat. "Ladies, we'll discuss this at a more appropriate time." He turned to Gabe. "Was there something else you needed, Detective?"

Clearly, Mr. Worthington didn't want a witness to the family drama. "I need to speak with Kris in private for a moment," Gabe explained.

"Anything you have to say to *Kristina* can be said

right here," Mr. Worthington replied in a voice that implied he was in control.

"Actually, sir, I can't. It's private."

"Are you and my daughter seeing each other?" Mr. Worthington demanded.

"Dad, please. Enough. My love life is none of your business."

"I beg to differ," her father corrected. "Are you dating Detective Burke?"

"No," Kris said, her voice wavering.

Mr. Worthington pinned Gabe with a fierce look. "Then what are you two doing together?"

Faced with the pointed question, Gabe sought Kris's gaze.

What had he gotten himself into?

Kris's stomach dropped. Gabe was going to bolt, just like last time. He had that same trapped, itchy expression as the night he'd broken up with her. Anger formed a knot in her chest. She had to get him out of here and fast, before her parents alienated him further.

"She needed a ride," Gabe answered.

Turning a disapproving frown onto Kris, her father said, "You should have called us."

"Next time I will."

Hoping to divert the conversation, Kris said, "May I borrow one of your cars?"

Mom frowned. "What's wrong with your grandmother's? Did it break down?" Without waiting for an answer, she rolled her eyes. "I knew it. We should have insisted you have a new car and not use my mother's ancient model." She threw her husband an irritated look. "Charles, we need to get Kristina a new car right away."

Kris sighed, hating that this old argument had to surface. Ever since she'd returned from Europe, her mother had been on her about driving Sadie's car. "Mom, I don't need a new car. Sadie's car is fine for me. It's being serviced."

Like getting four new tires. Not that she was going to tell them as much or why the tires needed to be changed out. She didn't want them to worry or interfere any more than they already had. If they knew what was happening, they'd yank Sadie from Miller's Rest and the mystery of the missing residents would go unsolved.

She slid a glance at Gabe. No, he wouldn't give up on the missing people.

But he gave up on you, a nasty voice in her head whispered. She resolutely shook the thought away. The past was the past.

"Never mind about the car. I'll just rent one," Kris decided. "Can you give us a ride to the rental place?"

"I have a ride coming," Gabe interjected. "Angie's on her way."

"Oh, well, good then." Why did she feel this burst of jealousy? Angie was his partner, not his girlfriend. At least Kris didn't think she was. She remembered the assessing way Angie had studied her. At the time she'd thought the scrutiny had been a cop thing, but maybe it was a woman thing.

Didn't matter. Not her concern.

Right, an inner voice mocked.

Gabe had intervened on her behalf with her parents

by saying they had plans for next Saturday. What was up with that? Did it mean anything to him?

She had to find out because the gesture meant more than it should for her.

"Of course, you can borrow a car. No need to rent one. I'm glad to see you are being responsible. Car maintenance is very important," her father said, rare approval in his tone. "You'll find the keys in the cabinet by the garage door. Take the Volvo."

Pleased by her father's offer, she went to give him a hug. "Thanks, Dad."

She gave her mother a hug, as well. As she pulled back, she said, "And, Mom, we are not attending the fundraiser."

Her mother sniffed in disapproval.

Kris moved to stand beside Gabe. "Walk me to the garage?"

"Of course," he said and extended his good arm. "Mr. and Mrs. Worthington." He acknowledged each with a nod.

Since she didn't want to embarrass herself any more than she already had in front of Gabe, Kris chose to ignore her mother's frown and the pensive expression on her father's face as she led Gabe from the room.

Taking the key from the cabinet, she pushed open the door leading to the garage and preceded Gabe out. She hit the automatic door opener and moved past her father's red Jaguar coupe and the big black Mercedes, to unlock the metallic gold Volvo. She opened the door but didn't climb in. Leaning on the car door, Kris searched Gabe's face and asked, "So what did you mean about Saturday night?"

His eyebrows twitched downward as if caught off guard. "Sorry. Didn't mean to open my mouth like that. It just sort of popped out."

Disappointment spiraled all the way to her toes. "Oh. Okay. I understand."

His frown descended into confusion. "You do? What do you understand?"

"That you only said what you did to get my parents off my back. I appreciate it." But she still didn't like having her hopes raised only to be dashed.

"I don't make a habit of lying and I'm not going to start now. If you're not busy, we'll do something that night."

"Really?" Anticipation and excitement bubbled, making her feel a bit giddy. "I'm not busy. I'd like that. A lot."

A horn beeped. Angie's brown sedan sat idling at the end of the driveway. Gabe waved to her.

A dart of jealousy made Kris tighten her grip, the sharp edges on the keys digging into her palm. *Get over yourself,* she silently chided. *He wouldn't be taking you out on Saturday if he and his detective partner were involved.* At least she hoped he wasn't the type to date more than one woman at a time.

She eased her grip and turned her focus back to the threat hanging over them. "So what now? How do we find Denise?"

Gabe arched an eyebrow. "*We* don't. I do. I'll let you know if anything develops." His worried gaze shifted to the keys in her hand. "Actually, that's why I wanted to talk to you privately. I really think you need to stay here at your parents'."

Indignation burst through her. "Excuse me?"

He held up his hands, palms out. "I know, not the ideal situation. You don't want to be back under your parents' control and I get that. I really do. But as much as I'd like to, I can't take you home with me, so this is the safest place for you."

Kris couldn't believe what she'd just heard. "You'd like to take me home with you? To your place?"

He flushed, red creeping up his neck. "To keep you safe. Someone obviously is going to great lengths to scare us off the trail of the missing residents. I don't know how far they'll go. Your parents have a high-tech security system. You'll be safe and I can concentrate on finding the bad guys."

She understood his point. Even agreed with it. She wasn't a martyr. "I can't tell them what's happening. How do I explain my sudden need to stay the night?"

"You can tell them part of the truth. Your apartment was vandalized."

She let out a short scoff. "Right. Like they wouldn't hire movers within ten seconds of the words leaving my mouth. That would just give them the impetus to put me under their thumb. I'm thirty years old. I don't want my parents' interference."

He conceded her point by inclining his head. "Okay, then tell them you wanted to spend some time with them. That since your car is in the shop and it's already so late in the day, you want to spend the night."

She turned the keys in her hands as his words turned over in her mind. The explanation sounded reasonable, though she knew they'd be suspicious because it didn't sound like her. But the thought of being alone in her apartment, in the dark, while someone out there wanted her dead scared her silly. And since most of her closet space in her apartment was taken up with photography paraphernalia, she did keep some clothes here.

She shut the car door. "Okay. For tonight at least."

"In the morning I'll have a patrol car meet you at your apartment. You don't go in until he has secured the premises."

Her mouth lifted on one side. "So I have to check in with you in the morning?"

"Yes. Unless you want to decide now on a time you'll be home."

She thought for a moment. It had been a long time since she'd had Camilla's eggs Benedict. The Worthingtons' cook was a rare find. "I'll be at my place by nine."

His relieved expression softened the hard lines around his eyes. "Thank you. And stay out of my investigation."

She gave him a droll look.

His gaze narrowed. "I mean it, Kris. No more snooping around, following people, asking questions. That's my job."

Considering the day's events, she really should agree, but passivity rankled her. "I'll try."

He shook his head. "That's as close to a promise as I'm going to get, isn't it?"

She shrugged. "I don't believe in making promises I'm not sure I can keep."

"That's an admirable trait," he stated with approval in his green eyes.

She preened slightly under his praise. "Thanks."

"I gotta go." He backed away.

Before he could take more than a few steps, she said, "I do have one question though."

"Yes?"

She stepped close to him, close enough to see the way his pulse beat at the base of his throat, close enough to feel the warmth of his breath as he regarded her a bit warily. "*Why* did you really say we were going out on Saturday night?"

"I—" He swallowed, his Adam's apple bobbing. "Because—"

"Yes?"

His gaze dropped to her lips. Her breath hitched as he suddenly lowered his head and kissed her. A breath-stealing, mind-blowing kiss that left her reeling when he broke contact.

"Call if you need anything," he stammered and then hurried down the driveway to join Angie in the sedan.

She stood there for several minutes after the car rolled away, letting the late afternoon chill seep through her coat. But she wasn't cold. Touching her fingers to her lips, she couldn't stop the smile or the welling of joy bubbling to the surface, warming her from the inside out.

He'd kissed her.

And now she couldn't wait until Saturday night.

Providing the bad guys didn't get to her first.

EIGHT

Gabe fastened his seat belt and glanced at his partner. She eyed the sling and thick bandage on his upper bicep. "You okay?"

"Yeah, thanks."

"You're a mess."

He nodded. *In more ways than one.*

She sighed and focused straight ahead as she drove, her black leather gloved hands at ten and two. She didn't say anything more though she must have seen him kissing Kris. He was glad for Angie's silence. He couldn't have explained the kiss anyway. To her, or himself.

So much for unemotional.

But Kris had stood so close, staring up at him with those big blue trusting eyes, asking him to explain about their supposed date. His actions defied reason.

Kissing her had been the wrong move. There was no future there, so why had he?

Because even after all this time, he wasn't as over her as he'd thought.

Too bad.

His feelings for Kris were immaterial. Kris wanted

love, something he didn't believe in, couldn't believe in. Love wasn't real. And what he was feeling for Kris was just attraction, anyway, nothing more. He couldn't allow it to be more. He scrubbed a hand over his face. He had to stay focused. Concentrate on the job at hand. He'd been grazed by a bullet today, for crying out loud.

Someone wanted them to stop digging into the disappearances at Miller's Rest, going so far as to make an attempt on their lives. That made him mad.

Anger could be a productive catalyst to solving this mystery.

"I need to go to the station and run all the retirement center's staff as well as the residents," he said, his mind going over the events of the past few days as he pulled out his notebook.

First, two people go missing. Carl Remming and Lena Street. Whereabouts unknown. Director's explanation; supposedly on vacation, unconfirmed. Then Frank, the janitor, was seen handing over pharmaceuticals on the street. Unable to substantiate a crime. No charges pressed.

A threatening note was written on Kris's apartment door. Then Denise Jamesen disappeared. Kris's tires were slashed. Someone shot at him and Kris on the way to verify the woman's supposed location. Not at relative's as the center's director claimed.

Was the director doing something with the missing people? And if so, what and why?

"I especially want to dig into Ms. Faust. Something is not right there," he guessed.

"Way ahead of you," Angie stated as she deftly drove

through late afternoon traffic toward the station house. "I already have the paperwork in the pipeline for a warrant to subpoena the personnel and residents' files. They should be in the house by tomorrow morning."

"Good. You're the best," he noted, grateful for her thoroughness.

"Right. The best," she muttered.

He chose to ignore the twinge of…he wasn't sure what he heard. Disappointment, cynicism?

Angie's cell phone rang.

"Carlucci."

She listened for a moment. "On our way."

She hit the siren and stepped on the gas.

Gabe settled back, half listening as Angie filled him in on a homicide at Fenway Park.

His mind kept going back to that kiss.

What had he been thinking?

The next morning Kris awoke from a restless night's sleep. She kept reliving Gabe kissing her. Kept seeing the expression of yearning in Gabe's eyes as his head dipped and his lips touched hers. Then only sensation. Warm, wonderful and full of tender hope.

Why had he kissed her?

Why had he promised to take her out on Saturday, even after she'd let him off the hook? To renew their relationship, go beyond a professional one?

She couldn't guess and was afraid to wish. Getting hurt wasn't something she wanted to repeat.

Before climbing out of bed in the room she'd grown up in, she reached for her old Bible, which Sadie had given her for her twelfth birthday. The tattered leather binding and soft pages filled her with nostalgia. The age at which reason and logic began to meld in a child's mind. When her faith took root.

She'd cherished the book and the words, especially after Sadie had convinced her parents to let her attend a youth group instead of attending the formal service in her parents' big monolithic church in downtown Boston.

Though as an adult, Kris didn't mind occasionally attending her parents' church. The architecture alone inspired awe and the pastor's messages were sound, but she felt most connected to God when she and Sadie attended the small rural church outside the city limits.

As was her custom since leaving home to live on her own, every morning she prayed for God to speak to her through His word. She had recently started reading Ephesians. She turned to the third chapter and scanned the verses until she came to where she'd stopped reading in the Bible by her bedside table in her apartment.

She began to read from verse fourteen through twenty-one. Her breath held as the words reverberated deep inside her soul. The passage talked of the power of the Holy Spirit and the desire the author, Paul, had for everyone to comprehend the vast greatness of God's love.

An ache gripped her chest as words spilled out.

"Please, Father, this is exactly my prayer for Gabe. That he would see how much You love him, that You haven't turned Your back on him. Please, soften his heart toward You. Let him cry out to You and show him that You care."

She bit her lip, then confessed, "And, Lord, I really like him. Even more than I did before."

Gabe was different than he'd been years earlier, and yet, not. Even then she'd known he was kind, courageous and intelligent. Now there was a compassion in him that hadn't been there before. Probably from years on the job. He exuded strength and reliability. A man of honor and integrity.

A man she could count on.

Who'd kissed her. But still the same man who had walked away from her eight years ago.

Give me strength, Lord, to leave the past behind once and for all.

Would *her* wound ever heal?

Like the wound inflicted on Gabe by a bullet meant for her?

A shiver of terror jetted down her spine.

When I'm afraid I will trust in the Lord. The words became a mantra to chase away the fear.

Feeling spiritually equipped, she set the Bible aside and readied herself for the day. She dressed in a pair of soft straight-leg jeans and a comfy cream-colored, cable-knit sweater. After a wonderfully prepared breakfast and a surprisingly amenable hour with her parents that didn't include any recriminations for not giving in to her mother's demand that she attend the upcoming fundraiser, Kris pulled the Volvo out of the garage and headed toward her apartment.

As she tuned the radio to a contemporary Christian station, she glanced in the rearview mirror. Her breath caught. A white van followed closely behind. The driver wore a baseball cap pulled down over dark sunglasses. It couldn't be the same van she'd seen at the retirement center three nights ago, could it?

Traffic forced her attention to the road.

She turned down her street. There was no police cruiser waiting to meet her. She glanced in the rearview mirror again. The van made the turn and continued to follow.

Stepping on the gas, Kris zoomed past her apartment. Keeping one hand on the steering wheel, she used the other to fumble through her purse for her cell phone. Seeing a side street, which would take her back the way she'd come, she yanked hard on the wheel and took the turn with a faint squeal of tires.

Nearly frantic, she shot another glance in the rearview mirror. The van was no longer behind her. Tension eased in her tight shoulders. She released her hold on the cell. She was just being paranoid.

Deciding she was safe, she rounded the corner to return to the street she lived on and parked in front of her building.

The van may not have been following her at all. The guy could have been just going in the same direction.

But they had been shot at just the day before. The memory slammed through her mind, causing a ripple of fresh anxiety. She grabbed her cell and called Gabe. It went directly to voice mail. She hesitated a moment before simply asking him to call her when he had a second.

When I'm afraid I will trust in the Lord, she repeated silently.

She refused to live her life in fear. Fear did not come from God.

Just as she stepped out of her car, a white and blue Boston Police car pulled up behind her. She blew out a relieved breath. God was good and He provided for those in need.

An officer climbed out of the car, introduced himself as Officer Barrett, and then led the way inside. Kris stood in the hallway outside her apartment as Barrett disappeared inside to check for hiding bad guys. When he returned, he declared all was clear.

"Detective Burke told me to tell you not to leave until you hear from him," Barrett said before exiting the apartment.

Smothering the irritation the officer's words evoked, Kris reminded herself she had to trust Gabe. He was concerned for her safety.

Grateful to have work to do while she waited for word on the investigation, she got busy. Her clients wouldn't be thrilled to know she'd let her personal life interfere with their projects.

In her studio, she spent the next couple of hours sorting through hundreds of photos and arranging them in a flowing scheme. The client, a landscape artist, had hired her to take pictures of his work from various job sites over the past three months for his brochures and Web site. Now all she had to do was mark the photos and send them off for the client's perusal.

Though she sent the photos in a file via the Internet, she also ran off hard copies. As she sealed the large envelope, her phone rang. She sprang out of her chair to grab the receiver. Hopefully it was Gabe. She longed to hear his voice. She had to repeatedly force herself not to call to check on the progress of his investigation. She was trying to let him do his job. She just wished he'd hurry up already.

She checked the caller ID. Sadie.

"Hello?"

"Krissy?"

Something in Sadie's tone made Kris's stomach clench with apprehension. *Please, God.* She didn't finish the prayer because she knew He knew her heart. "Are you okay?"

"Yes, dear. Just very tired today. I was hoping you could come visit. It's been too long since I last saw you. I get so lonely here sometimes."

Dread seized Kris by the throat. Sadie spoke as if she hadn't seen Kris in weeks rather than just yesterday. And she did sound weary. "I'll be right over," she promised, even as a worried little voice inside her head reminded her that Gabe had asked her not to leave until she'd heard from him. She pushed the thought away. He'd only said that because he wanted her to stop treading on his investigation. Visiting Grams didn't constitute snooping.

She decided to drop the envelope off at the client's downtown office before heading to Miller's Rest. But maneuvering through traffic took longer than she'd expected. Anxiety mounting, she called the client's office to ask the receptionist to come out to receive the package of photos so Kris wouldn't have to find a place to park.

Once the pictures were delivered, Kris wound her way through the late morning traffic and onto the highway leading toward Miller's Rest.

Outside, snow began to fall in big, fluffy flakes. Her windshield wipers had trouble keeping up with the deluge falling from the sky.

She concentrated on the road ahead.

Suddenly, a bump jarring enough to pitch her body forward shuddered through the vehicle. She gasped as her nose barely missed slamming into the steering wheel. Had she run over something?

A quick glance at the rearview mirror sent a chill of terror raging through her. The white van from before was behind her, so close she couldn't see the bumper.

Oh, Father, help me.

She sped up. He did, too.

Panic slicked her hands on the steering wheel. She adjusted her grip the best she could. She knew from having driven this road so many times that up ahead the road curved and on the right side the ground gave way to a deep ditch.

The van moved over into the oncoming lane and drew alongside her car. Oh, no! He was going to push her off the road.

"Lord, help me. What do I do?" Her voice bounced around the interior of the car.

Lightning fast, a plan formed. She didn't hesitate to examine or analyze, simply acted.

With one hand, Kris grabbed the emergency brake and pulled just as both feet stomped down hard on the brake pedal. The car slipped and skidded a few feet as the Volvo's ABS brakes fought to do their job. The car came to a screeching halt. The van shot past her and barely missed her front bumper as it veered into her lane. With tires spitting up snow, the van skidded around the turn then disappeared out of sight.

She let go of the e-brake, cranked the wheel to the left and punched the gas, sending the coupe sliding into a semicircle so that she was facing the other direction. She pressed the gas and sped toward the city as fast as the falling snow would allow, the whole while checking her rearview mirror for the van.

Tears of relief and panic slid down her cheeks.

"Thank you, God. You're awesome."

There was no doubt in her mind He'd just saved her. And she suspected some of Gabe's quick thinking was rubbing off on her. She sent up a prayer of thanks for bringing Gabe back into her life.

She looked for her cell phone but it must have slid to the floor.

As she entered the city limits, she slowed and drove directly to the Boston Police Department. She parked in the front and searched the backseat floor until she finally found her cell phone wedged under the passenger seat. With trembling fingers, she dialed Gabe's number.

Hopefully he was there and could come out so she didn't have to go in. She felt safe locked inside the car. The voice mail picked up on the third ring. Disappointment and panic made her voice wobbly. "Gabe, I need you to call me ASAP. I was on my way to visit Grams—" Her sentence broke on a sob. "Call me."

Not sure what else to do, she ran inside the police department, her knees shaking.

"Can I help you?" an older, uniformed man behind the

front desk asked. He was the same officer who'd escorted her to Gabe the last time she'd come to his work.

"Detective Burke," she managed to say. Her heart was beating so fast, she was having trouble catching her breath. Her hands were quivering. She jammed them into her coat pockets.

"He's out on a call. Can someone else help you?" He searched her face, concern etched in the deep lines at the corners of his brown eyes.

"I don't…" She felt slightly dizzy. She grabbed the desk for support.

"Miss, are you all right?" He came around to her and led her to a chair. "Sit here. Let me get you a glass of water."

Kris put her head between her knees to stop the spinning.

Someone had tried to run her off the road. Tried to kill her. Again.

She had to find Gabe. What if he were in danger, too? Oh, no. Grams! What if that van headed to the center? What if whoever wanted her to stop looking for the missing people did something to Sadie? Fresh panic halted her breathing. She concentrated on filling her lungs and slowly letting the air out as the world continued to spin.

When the officer came back bearing a plastic cup of water, she straightened to ask, "Is there any way to contact Detective Burke?"

"I can have Dispatch reach him." His bushy white eyebrows drew together in concern. "Are you sure no one else can't help? You're awfully pale."

How could she begin to explain? "No. I need to go."

She had to get to Sadie. She raced out of the building and to her car.

Behind the wheel with her hand on the ignition, she froze. Did she dare drive the same car back toward Miller's Rest while that van was still out there?

What were her options?

Sit tight and wait for Gabe to call. Or go to her parents and use one of the other cars to drive to the center, hoping she arrived before the van? Not likely.

She cringed at the thought of facing her parents with this information but decided she would have to tell them what was going on eventually. They would want to know why their car was all banged up.

Fear for Sadie wormed through her mind. She yanked out her cell phone and dialed Sadie. The phone just rang.

Shaking with thoughts of horrible things that could be happening to Sadie, Kris called the retirement center.

"Miller's Rest Retirement Center," said the receptionist in a soothing voice.

Kris could picture the pretty brunette. "This is Kris Worth, Sadie Arnold's granddaughter. Could you please connect me with her nurse?"

"I'm sorry. The residents don't have private nurses. Let me see who is on duty. Just a moment please."

Muzak filled the phone line while Kris waited; her heart pounded in her chest, making her ribs ache. The cold air bit into her skin. She started the engine and cranked up the heat.

"Miss Worth, this is Nurse Cathy, how can I help?"

"I really need you to check on my grandmother. She called me earlier and didn't sound…normal. I just want to make sure she's all right."

"I saw Sadie in the common room with the other ladies having tea barely five minutes ago. She seemed perfectly fine to me. Would you like me to have her call you?"

Relief oozed over her frayed nerves. "Actually, yes. That would be great. Also, could you keep an eye on her? Make sure she isn't left alone."

"Okay. I can do that. Is everything all right?"

"I'm just worried about her."

"Very well."

Kris hung up. Okay, Sadie was safe. For now. She turned off the engine and went back inside the police station. She could at least get the ball rolling on finding out who owned the white van.

"Unbelievable!" Charles Worthington proclaimed as he stared at Kris. "You're saying someone deliberately tried to run you off the road. And yesterday someone took a shot at you? Is that how Burke got injured?"

Cringing, Kris nodded. "Yes."

"Oh, my poor baby." Tears welled in her mother's eyes as she put one hand to her mouth as if to keep from throwing up.

Kris grimaced. Her parents were taking the news as she'd expected. Her father with righteous anger and her mother with worry that any moment would turn into smothering concern.

They were gathered in the living room. Kris and her mother were seated on the couch, her mom looking regal in a red sweater, pearls and black wide-leg pants. Her father paced in front of the fireplace, his blue oxford button-down dress shirt as crisp as if he'd just put it on rather than having come home from his office after a day of managing the family's wealth.

"The police are searching for the van right now and I had a police escort here. I'm fine. Gabe will be stopping by as soon as he can," Kris detailed.

She'd finally connected with Gabe via cell phone. He'd had a long night at a crime scene and she'd felt bad telling him of her near-death collision but his distress and anger warmed her. She didn't doubt he cared about her safety. But did he care about her in other ways? She really, really hoped so.

A look passed between Meredith and Charles. "We can't rely on the police to keep you protected," her father said.

Kris's own gaze narrowed. "We can't?" Kris plucked at the collar of her sweater. It was hot in the house, especially under her parents' scrutiny. "I trust Gabe to put a stop to this."

But the real question was, was she brave enough to trust him with her heart?

"I'm sure they'll do the best they can, but you can't expect the city police to assign someone to be with you at all times. It's just not feasible," Charles explained.

She had relied on Gabe more than was reasonable. She couldn't keep monopolizing his time, no matter how much she'd like to. "Of course not."

"Do you know why this is happening?" her mother asked.

"Maybe," she hedged. How did she explain? She might as well just get it over with. She braced herself for their reaction. "I think it might be because…" She swallowed. "Well, see, there have been some residents from Miller's Rest who have, uh, gone missing. And I've been trying to find them."

"Missing?" Her mother's voice rose an octave.

"What?" Her father's voiced deepened. "You've been trying to find them? What exactly do you mean?"

"I've been asking questions. Following Frank, the center's janitor. Going to visit one of the missing people's relatives," she confessed. It was better to get it all out in the open now rather than later in bits and pieces.

Her father ran a hand through his still-thick silver-flecked hair. "This must stop. You must let the police do their job." He pinned her to the couch with a stare. "And Burke knows all of this?"

Uh-oh. "Uh, well, yes, but he—"

"Unbelievable. I'm going to fry his—"

She jumped up. "No. He's been telling me to back off from day one. He doesn't like what I've been doing any more than you do. But even when he didn't believe anything bad was going on, he has been protective and kind to me and Sadie."

"Hmph. He should have told us when he was here yesterday," Charles countered, though clearly not appeased.

"I asked him not to," Kris declared.

Her father's irritated expression made Kris feel like a nuisance. She swallowed hard and straightened under his glare.

"What does my mother have to do with this?"

Meredith asked, her wide-eyed gaze a bit frantic. "She's not missing, is she?"

Redirecting her attention, Kris answered, "No. Grams is fine. She's the one who alerted me to the missing people."

"And what does the center say about these missing individuals?" Charles inquired.

Hiking a hip on the arm of the couch, Kris said, "The director has an explanation for every one of them."

Her father frowned and eyed her intently. "But you don't believe the explanations?"

She shook her head. "No. I don't."

Charles looked thoughtful for a moment. "Okay then."

"Okay?" Kris wasn't sure what he meant by that.

"An associate of mine, Gordon Trent, his eldest son is a personal security specialist. I'm going to call him right now," he stated and walked toward the door.

Meredith brightened. "Oh, good idea."

Annoyance shot through her as once again they were ready to barge forward, interfering in her life without so much as asking permission. "Wait. What do you mean 'personal security specialist'?"

"A bodyguard," her mother clarified.

Taken aback, Kris jumped to her feet. She didn't like the idea at all. "Really? That's a little extreme."

"Actually, it's a very good idea," came a familiar deep voice from behind her.

She whirled around to find Gabe in the arched doorway of the living room, his suit looking rumbled and his tie askew. He'd lost the sling but she could still make out the bulge from the bandages wrapped around his upper arm. He looked tired, but determined. She drank him in, wanting nothing more than to fly into his arms where she would be safe.

"You agree I need a babysitter?" Kris asked.

"You need protection," he said.

Right. A bodyguard to protect her person, but who was going to protect her heart?

NINE

Gabe walked forward to take Kris's hands, grateful to see her healthy and safe. The second he'd heard about the van trying to run her off the road, everything inside squeezed tight until his lungs were devoid of breath. He hadn't been able to take a full breath since until now. "Look, your parents are right to worry. And having you protected by a bodyguard would free me up to do my job."

Disappointment flashed in Kris's eyes. Gabe resisted the need to take her into his arms and tell her how important her safety was to him. How important *she* was. But with her parents watching, their disapproving gazes boring into him, he contented himself with giving her hands a gentle squeeze.

"Listen to the detective, Kristina," her father urged. "Let him do his job and find the person trying to hurt you."

Her mouth twisted. "And find the missing people."

"Of course. He can do that, too."

Kris took a deep breath and exhaled with a nod. "All right, Dad. Call Mr. Trent."

"Is my mother in danger?" Mrs. Worthington asked, her voice full of anxiety.

Gabe shifted his gaze from Kris's blue eyes to meet Mrs. Worthington's. "I can't say for sure. We haven't established that any crimes have been committed against the missing residents."

"But you're concerned," Mr. Worthington stated, somehow reading Gabe's feelings so easily.

Gabe nodded, surprised by his perception. "We have a BOLO out on the van that tried to run her off the road."

"BOLO?" Kris asked.

"Means 'be on the lookout.' The department dispatcher types the information you gave us in to NLETS—" Seeing her questioning look, he explained, "National Law Enforcement Telecommunications System. This is connected to NCIC, National Crime Information Center and is sent immediately to other agencies. It's our best chance of finding the van."

"Wow. I didn't think I had remembered enough to be helpful."

"Hey, you got the first two letters of the license plate and gave a good description of the dents in the front. There can't be that many white panel vans matching what you've given us. We've had success with less."

She looked pleased. "Good."

Wanting to make sure she didn't become complacent about her or Sadie's safety, he said, "But until we find this guy, I would feel better if Sadie was removed from Miller's Rest."

Kris pulled her hands out of his. "You can't take Grams away from her friends. She likes it there."

"It would only be temporary," he assured her.

"But where would she go? I'm not set up at my place

for her. She couldn't manage the stairs. And she'd feel trapped," Kris explained, her growing agitation evident with every wave of her hand emphasizing her words.

"She'll come here, of course," Mrs. Worthington asserted, her tone reflecting her indignation that Kris suggested otherwise.

Kris faced her parents. "What? I thought you wanted her where you wouldn't have to deal with her. You never visit her. Rarely ask her to visit you."

Her mother looked hurt. "I've never wanted her anywhere but here. *She* didn't want to live with us. And believe me, I pleaded and begged for her to move in here but she said she'd rather spend her time with others her age. I tried visiting in the beginning, but she'd get so agitated. The center director thought it would be better if I didn't come unless my mother invited me. She never has." Mrs. Worthington's voice broke. "I've never cared for that place she picked. Not when there is a much nicer one closer to us."

Kris's anger visibly left her. Compassion filled her expression. "Oh. I didn't know. Why didn't you tell me?"

"The director asked you not to visit?" Gabe asked, growing more and more certain Ms. Faust was up to something.

Mrs. Worthington gave a delicate shrug. "She said upsetting Mother wasn't good for her. Ms. Faust suggested having Sadie come here for visits, but the few times we tried were a disaster. Mother didn't like the food or the house was too hot or too cold." She shook her head. "I was so thankful when Kris returned from Europe. Mother was on her best behavior when Kris brought her over."

Kris moved to sit beside her. "I'm so sorry. I just didn't know. I thought—" She made a helpless gesture. "I'm afraid Grams's mind is…" She took a deep breath, hating to even admit it but she had to. She had to start coming to terms with the fact that Sadie's mind was slipping. "Dementia is setting in."

Sadness entered her mother's eyes as she lifted a trembling hand to her mouth.

"I don't know how Grams will take living here," Kris stated.

"Believe me, we have no illusions. She'll hate it. But we're family. We take care of our own," Mr. Worthington stated, putting his hand on his wife's shoulder.

Gabe swallowed back the rising emotion churning in his gut. The Worthingtons were turning out to be so different than he'd remembered. And different from the way Kris described them. Seeing how they were pulling together made him ache like he hadn't since he was a child and had watched other kids with their parents. He'd longed to have a family with a mom and a dad. Parents who cared. Parents who were involved.

He'd had his mom and a slew of "daddies" over the years, but only one had ever shown any genuine interest in Gabe. Officer Mark Peets. Gabe had idolized him. But he'd been killed in the line of duty.

Gabe had stood by the grave and vowed never to let himself get that close to anyone again. Doing so hurt too much.

Peets's death left Gabe's mother to weep alone, then search again for true love. She was always searching for true love, and was still alone.

Guilt sneaked its way into his mind. When was the last time he'd contacted his mother? Checked on her?

Long enough that he couldn't remember. Shameful.

He made a mental note to call her later, after he had Kris situated.

Mrs. Worthington stood up. "The downstairs room will need to be readied. We could put a door between the guest room and the bath to make her a private suite. She'd like that. It might make it more tolerable for her. I wonder how fast the remodeling would take?"

"At least a couple of days," Mr. Worthington stated.

Gabe tuned into the conversation. He cleared his throat. "That wouldn't take care of the immediate safety issue."

Mr. Worthington inclined his head in agreement. "Then we'll get Sadie a bodyguard, as well."

"Oh, she'll like that," Kris quipped in a tone that suggested the opposite. She sighed. "Though I think she'd probably be more amenable to a babysitter than moving."

Mrs. Worthington's expression turned a bit sad. "You're probably right."

"Then that settles it," Mr. Worthington insisted. "I'll call Trent now and set it up." He exited the room.

"I should probably go tell Grams," Kris said as she stood.

Her mother patted her arm. "I agree. She'll take the news much better from you. But please invite her to come here. Besides, once she learns that you'll be living with us, she might be more agreeable."

Anger sparked in Kris's eyes. "Uh, I figured I'd go home to my apartment since I'll have my own babysitter."

Mrs. Worthington's expression turned stern. "Nonsense. Until the man who tried to kill you is caught, you'll stay here."

Kris flung a look at Gabe, her silent plea for him to intervene obvious. He could only nod his agreement with her mother. As much as it galled Kris to be under her parents' thumbs, Gabe had no doubt she'd be safest here.

She scrunched up her nose at him. "Fine. I'll sleep here only until this is over. But I still have work to do, so I'll be at my studio during the day."

Mrs. Worthington opened her mouth to reply, but Gabe interjected, "With the bodyguard in place, working at your apartment should be all right."

"Should be?" Mrs. Worthington intoned. She gave him a pointed look. "It had better be."

Gabe met Kris's mother's gaze dead-on. "She will be protected. I will make sure of that. You have my word."

She assessed him for a moment, her conflicted blue eyes seeking something. She must have liked what she found because she gave a sharp nod of her head. "Very well. I will trust you. I'm sure you will explain to the bodyguard how important my daughter's safety is."

"You can count on it," he replied.

"Thank you." Mrs. Worthington touched Kris on the arm as she passed her on her way out of the living room.

As soon as they were alone, Kris said, "That was so weird."

"How so?" Gabe asked.

"My parents. I mean, do I even know these people? Have I *ever* known them? I had no idea they'd wanted Grams to move in with them. I assumed—"

"You assumed the worst," Gabe gently finished for her.

Guilt flashed across her pretty face. "Yes. Why do I do that?"

He didn't have an answer, though he wondered about the validity of the assumptions he'd made about his mother.

"Can you take me to see Grams now?"

He smiled. "How did I know that was coming?"

"Because you're smart."

He snagged her elbow as she strode past him. She stilled. Her gaze lifted to his. "Thank you," he said.

Two little creases appeared between her pretty arched eyebrows. "Why?"

"For being willing to see how important you are to your family. And me."

She blinked. "I am?"

More than he could say. "Yes. And we *will* find the person behind the attempts on your life." He had the warrants for the personnel and resident files in the car. He didn't intend to leave Miller's Rest without the documents. He'd already called Ms. Faust, letting her know he was on his way. He expected the files to be waiting for him.

Kris's eyes narrowed slightly. "Right. Because that's your job." She tugged her elbow away. "Let me get my coat and purse. I'll meet you outside."

Then she disappeared up the stairs to the second floor. Not sure what to think of their last exchange or how badly he'd had to fight not to dip his head and kiss her again, Gabe headed for the front door.

"Detective Burke," Mr. Worthington called out as Gabe passed the study.

Gabe stopped in the doorway. "Sir?"

"Please, call me Charles," he said and waved Gabe in to the room. "Have a seat."

Gabe did as requested and sat in the armchair facing the desk. Was Mr. Worthington, uh, *Charles,* actually starting to approve of him?

"I appreciate the concern you have for my daughter," Charles said as he steepled his fingers on the desk.

Uh-oh, here comes the "you're not good enough for my daughter" speech. The speech Gabe had hoped to avoid eight years ago. So much for acceptance. Gabe braced himself.

"I know my daughter can be a bit impulsive and flighty," Charles mused in a tone rife with parental patience.

An assessment Gabe didn't agree with. The need to defend Kris rose sharply. "She's kindhearted and totally loyal, not to mention hardworking with a strong sense of purpose," Gabe countered, his voice gruff even to his own ears.

Charles smiled slightly, his intense gaze speculative. "Yes, she is that, too."

The urge to squirm under the man's scrutiny had Gabe's blood pressure rising. He wanted to loosen the tie suddenly choking him. He cleared his throat and fought to stay professional. "Were you able to secure a bodyguard for Kris? If not, I know several good retired officers who would be a good choice."

"Indeed." Charles sat back. "Trent Associates will be sending over a man later this afternoon. I'd appreciate you being here to meet the man and assess his worthiness."

Once again Gabe was taken aback by Mr. Worth—Charles's—request. Obviously he valued Gabe's opinion. Who would have thought? "Of course. Whatever I can do to help."

Gabe didn't need to turn around to know Kris stood in the doorway; maybe it was the soft powdery scent she wore that teased his senses or the fact that he was so attuned to the pattern of her walk or the slight *huff* she let slip when she was upset. How much of the conversation had she overheard? Heat ringed his collar. Had she heard him defending her?

Her father smiled. "Come in, sweetheart. Detective Burke and I were just discussing your bodyguard."

"Please, call me Gabe."

Charles acknowledged the courtesy with a nod.

"Really?" Kris said as she came to stand beside Gabe's chair. Her hip bumped against his shoulder. "And?"

"Gabe has agreed to interview the man Trent Associates is sending over."

She deliberately knocked against him. "I thought you were going to take me to see Grams?"

He glanced up at her. "I am. Right now." He turned back to Charles. "Your wife thought it would be best if Kris explained the situation to Sadie. We're going there now, and we'll return before the bodyguard arrives."

Charles's gaze jumped between the two. More speculation entered his gaze. "Hmm. Well, as long as Meredith has agreed."

Gabe felt Kris straighten. One glance at her face told him that she was going to let loose some retort about not needing anyone's permission. Abruptly, Gabe stood and put his hand to the small of her back. "If you'll excuse us, Charles."

The corner of his mouth tipped in amusement. "Of course. I know my daughter is in good hands. We'll see you both back here in a few hours."

Guiding Kris out of the house, Gabe could feel anger simmering in Kris's blood.

"My, you two became quite cozy," she jabbed as she slid into his vehicle.

"We have a common interest," he replied and started the engine.

She crossed her arms over her chest and stared out the passenger window as he drove through the city.

"Look, I know you don't like this situation, but it can't be helped. Staying at your parents' is the logical and most practical solution."

"I know," she said and sighed. She turned to face him. "It's just they treat me as though I'm still a kid. I hate it."

"Granted, they can be overbearing, but they do it because they love you. Besides, to them you are a kid. Their kid. That's never going to change. But you're in control of how you react. Which in turn might help change how they treat you."

She narrowed her gaze. "How I react?"

He flipped on the windshield wipers to combat the falling snow. "Instead of getting upset, reason with them. Explain how you feel."

Her lips curled upward. "You sound like my therapist. I know, logically, occasionally we all revert to our childhood roles when we're with our parents. But when

I get in the same room with them, all that head knowledge deserts me and I just…react."

His lips twitched. She did that with him, as well. "So I noticed."

She gave him a sharp glance. "Does your mother treat you like a kid?"

"No."

"You're blessed then."

He glanced at her. Not exactly. "When it comes to my mother, I'm the grown-up and she's the kid."

Kris didn't know what to say. He'd never really talked about his childhood. Pretty much all she'd gotten out of him years ago was that he didn't know who his father was. "Has it always been just you and your mom?"

He made a noise deep in his throat. "No. There've been a lot of potential fathers in and out of my life. My mom has been chasing love since…well, forever. She doesn't live in reality."

Thinking back to his comment that love didn't exist, she said, "You really don't believe in love?"

"No."

Sadness filled her. Sadness for her and Gabe's past, which apparently had been doomed from the beginning. She could now see that. And sadness that a future together wasn't possible. "And you don't believe God exists?"

He frowned. "I never said that."

"But you'd said you didn't believe in Him."

With a sidelong glance, he replied, "Totally different."

"How?"

"I know He exists. But believing that He cares about *me?* No. No way."

Her heart ached to think Gabe felt unloved by God. "Why would you think that?"

"You don't grow up the way I did and believe some supreme being cares about you. Especially now, after years on the job. I just think God helps a select few and the rest He's turned His back on."

His words were sharp barbs to her soul. The God she knew, the God of the Bible, wasn't like that. How had Gabe come to such a bleak outlook? She could only imagine the horrors he'd seen as a police officer, but his animosity went further back. Barely able to keep her tears of sorrow for the bitterness in his voice at bay, she managed to say, "How *did* you grow up? You've told me so little about your past."

"Doesn't matter."

"Does to me. You matter to me," she confessed even as heat flushed up her neck.

The wounded, wary expression in his eyes as he studied her had her holding up a hand to ward off his words. "I know. I know. You don't believe in love and I shouldn't fall in love with you again. Believe me, I have every word dialed in already."

He returned his gaze to the road ahead. His hands gripped and regripped the steering wheel. "Good to know."

The tone of his voice was odd, a strange mix of resignation and yearning. Not letting her curiosity be sidetracked, she moved forward with her quest to find out exactly what made him believe God had abandoned him. Because there had to be a way to convince him otherwise. "Please, tell me about your childhood."

"Seriously, there's nothing to tell. No big traumatic

incident, no abuse. No nothing. Just a single mom more interested in the fantasy of love than in her son."

"You must have felt very alone."

He brought the car to a halt in a parking spot outside Miller's Rest. He shifted to face her, his expression hard yet so painfully vulnerable. "Yes. It made me feel very alone. I have always been alone and will always be alone. Now, enough psychoanalyzing me. Let's go tell Sadie about the bodyguard."

Kris's heart ached for him as she followed him from the car. *Please, Lord, help me to make him see how much You love him.*

They found Sadie in her room in bed.

"Grams? Grams, are you awake?"

Sadie stirred, her eyelids fluttering open. "Oh, Krissy. I'm so tired today."

Kris shot a worried glance at Gabe. "This isn't normal."

"I'll find a nurse," he said and left the room.

Kris took Sadie's hand. Her skin felt clammy and cold. Kris touched her wrist to Sadie's forehead to determine if her grandmother had a fever.

"Grams, do you feel sick? Nauseous? Pain?"

Sadie shook her head. "No, dear. Just sleepy."

A red-haired nurse wearing green scrubs hurried in with Gabe on her heels. Kris moved aside to allow the nurse to check her grandmother's vitals with the stethoscope she removed from around her neck. Gabe stepped closer and put his hand low on Kris's back. She leaned into him, appreciating his support.

After a moment the nurse straightened, her gaze kind.

"She seems to be fine. Her temperature is a little low. Does she have another blanket?"

Kris found a thick fleece blanket in the closet and spread it over Sadie.

"It's okay for her to rest, if she feels the need," the nurse assured her.

Kris gave the woman a wan smile. Okay, maybe she'd worried unnecessarily, but with all that had happened, who could blame her? "Thank you for checking her," she said as the nurse left the apartment.

"Are you all right?" Gabe asked Kris, his tone reflecting concern.

She shrugged. "I guess I'm still a little shaken by what happened earlier."

"That's understandable." He gave her a quick hug. "I need to speak with the director. Why don't you explain what's going on to Sadie," Gabe suggested before he, too, left the room.

Missing his arm around her, Kris sat on the edge of Sadie's bed. Her grandmother looked so fragile lying there tucked beneath her covers. Her eyes had closed again. "Grams?"

Sadie opened her eyes. "Krissy, you're still here."

"Yes, I'm still here. I have something I need to tell you."

"Yes, dear?"

She hesitated, unsure where to begin or how much to reveal. Her mother's request that she at least offer their home to Sadie played in Kris's mind. "Grams, with all that's been going on, would you be willing to move to Mom and Dad's house?"

A small frown appeared between Sadie's eyebrows. "Why? Your mother doesn't want me there."

Her heart squeezed tight. "Yes, she does. Mom really does love you, Grams."

Sadie gazed at her patiently. "I know that. But she shouldn't have to care for me. I don't want to burden her like that."

"Oh, Grams, you're not a burden. No one thinks that. We just want you to be safe and well cared for."

"They take good care of me here."

Kris thought of Sadie's suspicions of the center's staff mere days ago. "We want you with us."

"Us?"

"I'm staying at Mom and Dad's for a few days."

"Why? I thought you liked your apartment."

"I do." Taking a deep breath and slowly letting it out, Kris knew she'd have to tell her the truth. "Grams, we think you might be in danger here. Someone doesn't want us to find the missing residents." Kris stopped short of telling Sadie about the shooting. "I'm worried they'll hurt you in the process. So Mom and Dad are going to hire a bodyguard for you until you can move into their house."

"Missing residents? Bodyguard?"

Kris's stomach squeezed tight. "Carl, Lena, Denise."

Sadie stared blankly at her for a moment. Kris's shoulders sagged with distress. Then Sadie's eyes widened. "Right. My friends. They're missing. Krissy, we have to do something. Call the FBI or something."

A measure of relief tingled through her. At least Sadie remembered her missing friends, if not the past few days. Maybe with prompting her memory would come back. "Gabe is helping us. Remember? He's a police officer."

A soft smile spread over Sadie's face. "Gabe. Such a nice young man. A keeper, that one."

A stab of longing hit Kris. Not a keeper for Kris. *I've always been alone and will always be alone.* His words ran through her mind like the teletype at the bottom of the TV news screen. Over and over again. Leaving no room for any argument.

The memory of their kiss rose to taunt her.

Surely there was hope that one day... She pushed away the thought. One kiss wasn't enough to build a dream on.

Only heartache lay in that direction. She couldn't change his mind. He'd made it clear love and God were not going to be a part of his world. Neither would she be after his job was done.

Yet she held out hope that God would one day win him over. Nothing was impossible for God.

For herself, however, there was no hope for a future with Gabe.

TEN

A knock on the door snagged Kris's attention away from her depressing thoughts. "Come in."

Mrs. Tipple entered the apartment. Today she wore a flowing long skirt and a soft tunic-style sweater. Her silver hair was unbound and hanging down her back. Kris hoped she'd still have a sense of style when she reached the older woman's age.

"Oh, excuse me. I didn't realize Sadie had a visitor. How are you, Kristina?"

"Well, thank you." She glanced at Sadie; her eyes had closed again and her breathing evened out. "Grams is resting."

"So I see." Mrs. Tipple smiled. "In that case, would you care for a cup of tea?"

A thought occurred to Kris. Though she'd already asked the woman about Denise Jamesen, maybe Mrs. Tipple might have some information on Carl Remming and Lena Street. It couldn't hurt to ask because Mrs. Tipple seemed to socialize with all the residents. "Tea would be great." Just in case her grandmother could hear her, she said, "I'll be back in a bit, Grams."

Kris followed Mrs. Tipple down the hall toward the independent living wing where the older woman's apartment was located. Mrs. Tipple chatted about the various residents as they went, pointing to each door with the nameplate and apartment number posted on the wall. Outside of each apartment were small shelves that the residents used as a porch of sorts. Some had potted plants or stuffed animals as cheery decor.

Toward the end of the hall a woman stepped out of an apartment. Kris recognized Vivian Kirk. Beside her Mrs. Tipple stiffened.

"Evelyn, I just peeked in to see if you were around," Vivian said with a broad smile as they approached.

"As you can see I'm not at home," Mrs. Tipple stated in a voice full of censure.

Belatedly, Kris realized the nameplate next to the door read Mrs. Evelyn Tipple. The term *nosey neighbor* came to mind.

"True." Vivian reached out to take Kris's hand in hers. "Hello, Kristina. How is your grandmother today?"

"A little under the weather."

Vivian's mouth turned down in an exaggerated frown. "Oh, that's too bad." She released her hand and cleared her expression. "I'll stop by to see her later."

"I'm sure she'd appreciate that," Kris replied. These ladies were very friendly. Maybe a bit too much?

"You were looking for me, Viv?" Evelyn reminded.

"Yes. I wanted to see if you were up for a game of tennis."

Kris stared at the elderly ladies. "Tennis?" The

weather outside was bitterly cold, not to mention the ground was covered with snow.

Vivian's eyes twinkled. "On the Wii in the game room."

"Ah." Now that made more sense.

"Ruth was supposed to play but she isn't feeling well today, either. There must be a bug going around, which isn't surprising considering the recirculated air."

"Thank you for asking, but Kristina and I were about to have a cup of tea. Care to join us?"

"You're too kind," Vivian said and then shook her head. "But no, thank you. Though, Evelyn dear, you are looking a bit dry today." To Kris, Vivian said, "Must keep hydrated in this forced, central-heated air."

Evelyn made an indelicate snort. "I'll keep that in mind."

Vivian flashed another smile. "I'll go rustle up another tennis partner. Maybe old George will take the challenge." She ambled down the hall and disappeared around the corner.

"She's a lively one," Kris commented.

"Yes, that she is. She's only fifty-seven, you know." Evelyn sighed. "To be that young again…"

Evelyn opened her apartment door and led the way inside. The small one-bedroom unit was decorated in soft pastels with watercolor prints on the walls, lace doilies adorning the antique-looking furniture and fresh flowers on every available surface.

"Your place is beautiful," Kris commented as she took a seat at the small, round dining table by the window that overlooked the courtyard.

"Thank you. I like it," Evelyn replied while setting

the teakettle to boil. Since Mrs. Tipple wasn't in the assisted living section of the center, her apartment was equipped with a functioning kitchen.

From a cupboard she brought down one of several glass jars full of loose tea leaves. She made a little tsking noise.

"Something wrong?" Kris asked.

"No. Just my memory. I keep leaving a filled tea ball in the jar." She dangled the filled mesh ball from the crook of her finger for a moment before setting the ball in a porcelain teapot. "I hope you don't mind lemongrass. I find it soothing."

Clueless about teas, Kris smiled. "Anything you choose will be fine." Though she'd have preferred some coffee for a little pick-me-up.

The kettle whistled. Evelyn filled the teapot with the steaming liquid. "We'll need to let it steep for a few moments," she said and sat down across from Kris.

Deciding to dive in with her questions, Kris asked, "Do you remember Carl Remming ever mentioning his vacation plans?"

Mrs. Tipple's eyebrows twitched. "No, can't say that I do. I know he's been gone for a while. He must like wherever he went." She smiled sweetly.

"What about Lena Street? She's supposedly on vacation, as well."

"Really?" Evelyn busied herself pouring tea into the small, delicate china cup in front of Kris. "I didn't know either of them well."

Something niggled at the back of Kris's memory. Something Sadie had said. Maybe the stress had more impact on memory than age. Great. Kris picked up her cup and sipped the hot liquid. The earthy flavor was pleasant and soothing as it went down.

Evelyn rose. "I think I have some scones left from yesterday. I use a diabetic recipe, hope you won't mind. I'll warm us up a couple."

"I didn't realize you were diabetic," Kris commented as she watched the fluid way the older woman bustled about her kitchen.

"You know as we age…" Evelyn let the sentiment hang in the air.

Kris nodded in understanding. So much changed as one grew older. Bodies failing, minds going. One day she'd be the elderly one. She could only pray that she'd have grand-children to visit with. To believe her if she said people were disappearing. But first she'd have to find a husband.

Gabe's face popped into her mind. And she willed the image away. No point in fantasizing about something that wasn't going to happen.

While Evelyn reheated the scones, Kris sipped her tea and turned her thoughts to what her grandmother had said about the missing people. They had been there one day and gone the next. No goodbye, no nothing. Gabe had looked at their rooms and found nothing to suggest foul play, which had to indicate they had left of their own accord. But Kris couldn't remember if he'd said their suit-cases were missing. She'd have to remember to ask him.

"Here we go," Evelyn announced as she settled a plate of two fluffy blueberry scones on the table.

"Thank you," Kris said and reached for a scone. She took a bite, expecting the scone to be dry and flavorless because of the dietary restrictions associated with diabetes, but the pastry was actually very tasty. Halfway through, though, her appetite deserted her as her stomache cramped. She put a hand over her abdomen.

"Are you all right? You're suddenly so pale," Evelyn observed.

Kris smiled even though her nausea surged and her chest tightened, causing her breathing to become a bit labored. "I don't feel so good. I think I should get back to Sadie." She stood, holding on to the back of the chair as the room tilted. A wave of heat swept over her and her body began to tingle. When the world righted, she moved toward the door. "Thank you for the tea and scone."

"Would you like to take the rest of your scone with you?"

Not really, but she didn't want to be impolite.

"That would be great."

Evelyn wrapped the pastry in a napkin and handed it to Kris. "I sure hope you don't have the bug that's going around."

"Me, too. I'm sorry to leave so abruptly."

Evelyn opened the door. "Not a problem. I've been fighting a queasy stomach myself lately. I hope you feel better soon."

Kris rushed out of the apartment and fled to Sadie's studio, feeling sicker by the second. Once inside, she deposited the scone on the table and hurried to the bathroom, where she promptly threw up. Once her stomach was empty and the dry heaves subsided, she rinsed her mouth and brushed some of Sadie's mint toothpaste across her teeth. Her lungs still hurt but her breathing had eased up. Had her breakfast turned bad? Or was her stomach upset due to the residual panic from earlier?

She said a quick prayer of healing before exiting the bathroom.

She found Gabe standing beside a still-sleeping Sadie. He turned and his expression grew concerned. "Whoa. You okay?"

Great, she must look as bad as she felt. "I just got sick," she explained and moved to sit in the rocker by the window. Her legs felt shaky and her mouth dry. "Would you get me a glass of water?"

"Of course," he said and went to the small sink. "Cups?"

"Cupboard to the right of the sink."

A second later, Gabe handed her a short glassful of cool water, which she gratefully drank. The liquid soothed her parched throat.

Gabe squatted down beside her, concern alight in the emerald depths of his eyes. "Should I get the nurse?"

She shook her head. "I don't think that's necessary. One of the residents mentioned a bug going around."

Looking unconvinced, he brushed back a strand of hair.

"Besides, it could just be stress. It's not like I was shot at or anything," she joked with a pointed look toward the bulky bandage beneath the sleeve of his suit jacket.

He rolled his eyes. "I just had a conference call with your father, Ms. Faust and Trent Associates. They are sending one of their people over right now, a woman by the name of Gina Tomes. I had Angie run her credentials. They checked out." He glanced at his wristwatch. "She should be here anytime now. She'll be posing as a full-time nurse for Sadie. Ms. Faust wasn't too pleased, but she really has no choice."

Relieved, Kris said, "That's good they can send someone so soon. Can we stay until she gets here?"

"Of course."

Her gaze strayed from his gorgeous eyes to her grandmother's sleeping form on the bed. "I know the nurse said Grams is okay but this is so unlike her to be sleeping during the day like this."

"But you did say Sadie wasn't sleeping well at night. Maybe the lack of sleep finally caught up with her? And she could have the crud that's going around."

Definitely a reasonable explanation, one she'd have to accept. For now.

To distract herself from Sadie, Kris asked, "Did you search the missing residents' rooms?"

"Angie did. She didn't find anything to suggest foul play. Lack of suitcases and empty hangers gave credence to Ms. Faust's vacation story."

"Did she ever give you their itineraries?"

He snorted. "As Ms. Faust repeated several times, this isn't a prison. Other than each resident making arrangements for their bills to be paid, not one left a number where they could be reached."

"So Ms. Faust really doesn't know what happened to the residents?"

With a shrug, he said, "Appears so."

A soft knock sounded at the door.

Gabe moved to open the door and admitted a stunning African-American woman, wearing a green nurse's smock over her dark pants and black turtleneck. Slung over her shoulder was a big, leather bag with balls of yarn and knitting needles poking out the top. Her long dark hair was swept back and held at the nape of her neck by a gold clip. Beneath her smock Kris detected a bulge that she guessed meant the woman was carrying a weapon.

"You must be Gina," Gabe said and stuck out his hand. "I'm Detective Burke."

"Glad to meet you," Gina said in a smooth voice.

Kris stood and met the woman's gaze. Gina's sharp, intelligent eyes assessed her. Kris held out her hand. "I'm Kris."

Gina took her hand, her touch warm and steady. "Hello, Kris. You won't have to worry while I'm here. I'll take good care of your grandmother."

Kris believed her. "Thank you."

Gina released Kris's hand. "I've been brought up to speed on the case," she told Gabe. "Another operative should be at the Worthington home by now."

"Good. Thank you." He handed her a business card. "If you need anything."

She pocketed the card. "Will do."

Gabe turned to Kris and held out his hand. "You ready?"

Her gaze bounced to Sadie even as her mind told her to trust that all would be well. God had Sadie in His care. "I suppose."

Her hand fit snugly within his grasp. A pleasant warmth spread up her arm, reminding her how good it felt every time he held her. Every time he touched her. Kissed her.

Reluctant to let go, she tightened her hold, refusing

to release him when his fingers slackened as they left the apartment. There may not be a future for them, but they had right now and right now she needed the contact.

She could feel his gaze searching her face as they walked toward the front of the center. He stopped as they neared the reception desk. "Ms. Faust has some paperwork for me," he declared to the receptionist.

"And she said you'd have something for her," the brunette countered with a smile.

"I do." Gabe pulled out an envelope from his inside coat pocket and handed it over.

The pretty brunette stared up at him with an amused glint. "Very good. Would you like help out with it?"

"Help out?"

The woman gestured toward a stack of boxes behind the desk.

"Oh, yes, I guess that would be good."

"Let me see where Frank is," said the receptionist as she dialed a number.

Gabe turned to Kris. "Feel up to carrying out a few boxes?"

She eyed the stack. "Sure. What are they?"

"Hopefully, the key to what's going on."

"That's cryptic," she muttered.

A few minutes later, Frank came walking down the hall. He stopped when he saw them. He started to back up. The receptionist called out to him. "Frank, come here."

Hesitatingly, he came forward, keeping his gaze pinned on Gabe. "Yeah?"

Kris thought the man was sneaky and not someone she'd trust, but apparently Gabe didn't share the sentiment.

"We need your help with these boxes," Gabe instructed, his tone even and unthreatening.

Frank's gaze jumped from the boxes to Gabe. "I guess I can help."

"Thanks, Frank, I appreciate it," Gabe said as he moved to the boxes. He handed one to Kris.

Frank hefted two boxes at once in his arms. "Where to?"

"The black SUV by the curb," Gabe indicated.

Frank carried the boxes out of the center.

"Are you sure about trusting him?" Kris whispered.

Gabe's gaze bored into her. "Trust *me*."

She did, probably more than she should. Because somehow when all was said and done, she knew her heart was going to pay a price.

Gabe immediately disliked the bodyguard Trent Associates had sent over to stand guard over Kris. It didn't matter that the guy's credentials were impressive—military-trained and college-educated. Or that he had glowing references from some major political figures and celebrities. The guy was capable and would protect Kris more than adequately.

There really wasn't any concrete reason for the burning dislike charging through his system.

Kris, on the other hand, seemed wowed by her new "babysitter" as she'd disparagingly referred to the bodyguard before she'd met the guy.

Through a narrowed gaze, Gabe watched the cozy way she talked with the man. He was closer to Kris's height than Gabe, he was smooth-talking, richly dressed and looked like some *GQ* ad. And his name, Donavan Cavanaugh. Sounded like a soap opera character. Ugh.

Charles Worthington pulled Gabe into the hall of their Beacon Hill home. Gabe positioned himself so he could keep an eye on Cavanaugh. Kris laughed at something the bodyguard said. Gabe's gut clenched.

"So what do you think?" Charles asked.

Forcing his mind and his gaze to center on Kris's father, Gabe contemplated demanding that Cavanaugh be sent away. But then he'd have to give a reason. Which he didn't have. Not really. Unless he admitted to the jealousy twisting his insides.

He was jealous. The realization knocked the breath from his lungs. He'd never felt any emotion so powerful before. How could he be jealous?

Ridiculous. He didn't do jealousy any more than he did love.

"He'll do." Gabe gave his stamp of approval in a terse tone. "I need to get back to the station. I have a stack of files to go through."

Charles's knowing smile only served to make Gabe more aware of how idiotic his feelings were. Good thing Kris hadn't witnessed his momentary bout with the green-eyed monster.

Jealousy was *not* part of the job.

Kris liked her bodyguard. He had a nice sense of humor and a congenial way about him that put her at ease. If she'd had a brother, Donavan could have fit the bill.

But judging by the thunderous expression on Gabe's face before he'd ducked into the hall with her father, she had the distinct impression Gabe wasn't so thrilled with him.

Interesting. Especially since he'd been all for hiring help earlier today.

When her father reentered the living room sans Gabe, Kris excused herself from Don and went to her father's side. "Where's Gabe?"

"He had some pressing work," her father replied.

She crinkled her nose. "He left? Without saying goodbye?"

The amused twinkle in her father's eyes made Kris's gaze narrow. "Why are you laughing at me?"

He gave her a rare grin. "No reason at all." And then quickly moved to speak with Don.

Kris knew what pressing work Gabe had to take care of. The files they'd brought with them from Miller's Rest. Hopefully, there would be something to lead them to her would-be killer.

By ten o'clock on Friday morning, Gabe had a crick in his neck and his eyes were dry from reading through several boxes full of Miller's Rest employee files. He sat at his desk, where he'd been all night. His back ached from his less-than-comfortable chair, his wounded upper arm throbbed and lack of sleep and caffeine was dragging his energy level into the pits.

And he still had several boxes with the residents' information left to go through, as well.

He pushed away from his desk and stood. Stretching muscles protested as he made his way to the coffeepot. Thankfully someone had brewed a fresh batch.

He poured himself a full mug and took a bracing gulp. Liquid fire heated him. Hot and black. Just like he liked it.

He checked with Dispatch to be sure there weren't any new cases demanding his attention. There weren't.

Grateful for that small favor, he went back to his desk. He'd reviewed the files on each employee, made a list of said employees to be entered into the NLETS. So far no hits coming back saying "bad guy." Even Ms. Faust checked out.

She seemed like a normal citizen. A college graduate earning a Masters in Science with an Eldercare concentration from some school he'd never heard of in the Midwest, a work history for the past twenty years in Scranton, Ohio, with glowing references before coming to the Boston area. No red flags there.

He'd only worked his way through half of the residents' charts but so far they appeared clean. Nothing to suggest some nefarious scheme going on. But even if a resident was involved, it would still take a staff member to dispose of the bodies.

If any bodies needed disposing. He rubbed a hand over gritty eyes.

They hadn't found any trace of the missing people. Maybe they had just left of their own accord and didn't want to be found?

Protocol mandated he turn the case over to the FBI's missing persons department.

But his gut instincts said the residents willingly leaving Miller's Rest seemed highly unlikely. They had a nice thing going there. Food, care, companionship. A medical staff 24/7. A dining room and planned outings. The residents paid a hefty price for such conveniences.

That thought gave Gabe pause.

Was money a factor in the disappearance of the three residents?

"Hey, Angie," he said, turning to his partner. "Did you subpoena the financials on the missing residents?"

She nodded and rooted around her desk for a moment before handing him a file folder. "Here you go. I haven't had a chance to go through them yet."

"Thanks. Would you be up for obtaining the financials for Miller's Rest?"

"Sure. I think it was included in the warrant so they might already be in one of the boxes." Her dark eyes regarded him with curiosity. "Where you going with this?"

"Not sure yet." He couldn't explain the nagging feeling that drove him. Looking at the account histories for Carl Remming, Lena Street and Denise Jamesen, they all had one thing in common: an automatic payment to Miller's Rest Retirement Center.

He stilled. No, they actually had a couple more things in common. All were roughly the same age and basically alone in the world.

Then something else snagged his attention. Carl Remming cashed a Social Security check two days after he went on "vacation" and then another check was made out to the center. Gabe flipped back to Lena Street's file. She, too, had a Social Security check cashed five days after leaving Miller's Rest and a few days later a check made out to Miller's Rest was paid.

No Social Security check or extra check to the retirement facility had been cashed by Denise Jamesen. Yet. But Gabe had a strong feeling that it would be only a matter of time.

"I need to find out who cashed these Social Security checks and who made out and cashed these other checks," he stated to Angie, handing her back the folder. "Can you follow the money trail?"

She gave him a pointed look that said, you're kidding, right? "Of course I can."

The phone on Gabe's desk rang.

"Burke."

"Hey, got a call you might be interested in," said Lily, the dispatcher. "Just received a 9-1-1 at Miller's Rest. Thought you'd want to take it. A woman's dead."

ELEVEN

Gabe's heart sank and dread filled him; a knot formed in his chest. "Do you have a name on the vic?"

"Yeah, uh, Palmer."

The knot loosened on a quick breath. "On my way."

Relieved that the fatality wasn't Sadie, he hung up and then gathered his gun, badge and overcoat as he filled Angie in on the call.

"The financials will have to wait." She retrieved her sidearm from the lockbox and holstered her weapon before grabbing a puffy down jacket from the rack next to her desk.

With the siren blaring, they sped to Miller's Rest. An ambulance and a couple of patrol cars were already on the scene. The ME's van arrived as they got out of their car.

Inside the center, the receptionist called out a room number and pointed toward the hallway on the left that led to the assisted living wing.

Gabe flashed his badge to the uniformed officers in the hallway before entering the studio apartment. Ms. Faust hovered near the bed as if still protecting her charge. Or was she the grim reaper? He just wasn't sure.

Her gaze acknowledged Gabe as he moved farther inside the studio apartment. An older gentleman wearing a doctor's coat stood talking to the paramedics. Dr. Crowley, Gabe presumed.

Though the space was similar in layout to Sadie's, this apartment was cheerless and sterile. No Christmas decorations, no family photos on the walls. The furniture looked like something one would find in a hotel. Very nondescript, generic. A gray-haired woman lay prone on the bed beneath a faded floral cover; her arms were crossed over her chest and her face in serene repose.

Angie began snapping off photos with the small camera she always carried. Taking out a notepad from his inside jacket pocket, Gabe recorded his observations. The door lock appeared untampered with, no signs of a struggle; in fact the place looked extremely neat, not even a layer of dust on the windowsill. A red flag waved. Had the room been wiped down to erase any fingerprints?

At first glance the whole setting suggested the woman's death was due to nothing more than natural causes. And if three other residents from this facility hadn't disappeared without a trace, he might be able to buy what the surface revealed.

As the medical examiner arrived to examine the body, Gabe turned his attention to Ms. Faust. "Who…?"

She swallowed. "Mrs. Palmer. Debra Palmer. She was such a sweet lady."

He vaguely remembered her file. A widow with no relatives. Another red flag went up in his internal warning system. "Who found her?"

Ms. Faust gestured toward the young blond woman talking with a male orderly. "Nurse Annie." She worried her hands. "Mrs. Palmer has burial instructions. I should go call the mortuary. How soon will she be released?"

"As soon as the ME has a cause of death," he replied. Strange that she wouldn't know that.

"Oh, right. I should still make arrangements," she repeated and hurried out of the apartment.

Gabe stared after her a moment. Her behavior was off. Did she already know the cause of death or didn't care to know?

"The ME says he'll rush the autopsy," Angie said, interrupting his thoughts.

"Good." He gestured to the blonde nurse. "Nurse Annie found her. Can you interview her? I'd like to ask the center's doctor a few questions."

With a sharp nod, Angie moved to talk to the nurse. Gabe snagged the doctor as he made his way out of the apartment. "Dr. Crowley?"

The man stopped midstride in the hallway. "Yes?"

Showing his badge, Gabe said, "Detective Burke. I have a few questions."

"Follow me to my office."

"Was Mrs. Palmer ill?"

"Not critically. Debra Palmer was hypertensive and had rheumatoid arthritis, but both were under control."

"Do you have a guess what caused her death?"

The doctor smiled. "Other than old age? No. Though I can't imagine her death was anything other than it was her time. It does happen that way sometimes. God only allots us all so many days on this earth."

"And sometimes a little help is given."

Opening the door to his office, the doctor gestured for Gabe to enter. "Are you suggesting, Detective, that I helped Debra to her end?"

Gabe shrugged noncommittally, hoping that if the doctor were guilty of something he'd trip himself up.

Dr. Crowley rounded his desk and sat in his chair. "I didn't."

"What can you tell me about Carl Remming, Lena Street and Denise Jamesen?"

"Well, now," the doctor said as he steepled his fingers, "you do realize doctor-patient confidentiality forbids me from discussing any patient's medical information with you?"

Gathering his patience, Gabe nodded. "I do. I want to know if you recall their plans before they left the center."

The doctor's bushy eyebrows rose. "Left the center?"

His surprise seemed genuine. "I take it you don't visit with the residents on a consistent basis."

"No, Detective. Unless a patient is in need of my services, I leave their medical care in the capable hands of the nursing staff. I share this position with another doctor. He may have more information than I do."

The other doctor hadn't had anything useful to say when Angie had interviewed him earlier in the week. "So none of the three in question mentioned going on vacation or visiting relatives to you?"

"I just stated I hadn't realized they'd left." He hesitated a moment. "But did you say Carl Remming?"

Gabe leaned forward. "I did."

Dr. Crowley's gaze grew concerned. "I do recall a

few weeks ago that he'd become violently ill. Ms. Faust had insisted he be transferred to the local hospital. He must have recovered and gone on vacation."

Gabe froze. "Maybe."

One thing was for sure, Ms. Faust had lied to him.

He said goodbye to the doctor and found Ms. Faust in her office. He walked in without preamble. "Why didn't you tell me Carl Remming had been taken to the local hospital?"

Ms. Faust's eyes widened. For a moment, Gabe was sure fear shone in the depths of her blue-gray eyes before she quickly found her composure.

"I hadn't thought it relevant. He'd been ill and for the health and safety of the other residents I had him taken to the hospital. They diagnosed a bad case of food poisoning. He recovered, returned and left on vacation. End of story." She gestured to the door. "Now, if you'll excuse me, I have a great deal of paper to contend with in regard to Mrs. Palmer."

"I'm sure we'll be talking again," he stated as he left her office. He went directly to Sadie's apartment. She didn't answer when he knocked. He tried the knob. Unlocked. He poked his head inside. She wasn't there.

Quickly, he made his way to the common area. Sadie and three other elderly ladies, one he recognized as Mrs. Tipple, sat drinking tea at a table near the fireplace. Relief eased the tension in his chest that he hadn't realized was there. He'd become more attached to Kris's grandmother than he'd thought possible.

Where was Gina?

Sadie's face beamed when she saw him. "Gabe, how wonderful of you to visit. Is Krissy with you?"

"Not today, Sadie," he replied and bent to kiss her soft cheek. "I came on official business but I couldn't leave without saying hello."

"Such a dear boy," Sadie said and patted his hand. "I told Krissy you were a keeper."

The gentle giggle of the three ladies only added to the heat rising up his neck. He could just bet what Kris's response was to that. Not a chance.

And she'd be right. Wouldn't she? They came from different worlds with different expectations. Yet, she'd changed over the years. Matured into a woman who wasn't dependent on life's luxuries for her happiness.

But the question was, could he get over his own issues of Kris's wealthy upbringing to forge a future with her? He didn't know. And wasn't sure he was willing to risk finding out.

Forcing his mind back to the elderly woman before him, he bent close to whisper, "Where's Gina?"

Sadie's eyes widened slightly with a conspiratorial gleam. With her head she indicated the far corner. Sure enough, Gina sat in a chair by the window knitting. She met Gabe's gaze and nodded.

Assured of Sadie's well-being, he said goodbye to the ladies, then made his way to the entryway where he met up with Angie. She drove them from the center in the sedan. Gabe was content to let her drive. He knew driving gave her a sense of control and right now he needed to relax so he could think.

"The CSI tech didn't find anything other than the vic's prints," she reported.

He'd figured as much. "Hopefully, the autopsy will reveal this was a natural death."

"But you don't believe that," Angie stated.

She knew him well. "No, I don't." He took out his phone and dialed Kris's apartment. The call went to voice mail. She was supposed to be at her studio working. He called her cell, same thing, straight to voice mail.

Worry gnawed at his gut. Had something happened to Kris? Had the death of the Palmer woman been a diversion?

Gabe didn't have Donavan's cell programmed in his phone so he had to hunt the man down through Trent Associates. Once he'd secured the correct number, he called, hoping that Kris was all right. And fearing what it would do to him if she weren't.

Kris spent the whole day safely ensconced in her work studio shooting an ad campaign for a trendy, local boutique while Don camped out in her living room acting both as doorman and bodyguard. The place had been filled with giggling models, a makeup artist, the store owner and racks of clothes. Kris was grateful to keep busy, but even with all the activity, she couldn't help worrying about Sadie. Or thinking about Gabe.

Was he following clues? Working on another case? Would he be all right at the end of the day?

She wondered how the wives of law enforcement officers lived each day knowing their husbands' lives were constantly at risk.

Finally, when the last of the clothes had been removed and the grateful owner had taken her leave, Kris collapsed on the couch, exhausted.

"You do this every day?" Don asked. He sat in a chair near the door. His dark chinos and long-sleeve turtleneck made him look more like a model than a specially trained bodyguard.

"No, thankfully." She smiled. "You sure were a hit with all the ladies."

The corner of his mouth tipped upward. "I hadn't noticed."

"Right." She didn't believe that for a moment. Though he hadn't paid much attention to the young models, Kris had noticed the way he'd watched Caroline Tully, the boutique owner. "Caroline's single. Just in case you were wondering."

He laughed. "I'll keep that in mind."

The phone clipped to his belt rang. He answered, his gaze darkening as it swung toward her. "Everything's fine here. Got it. Not a problem, Detective. I'll let her know."

Kris sat up straight, adrenaline and fear pumping through her heart. Was Gabe okay?

He hung up. "That was Burke. Your grandmother is okay but there's been a death at the center."

Relieved to hear that Sadie was well, but upset to hear that someone had died, she frowned. "Why didn't he call me himself?"

Don shrugged. "Said your phones all went to voice mail."

She slapped a hand to her forehead. "Right. Of course. I always set both phones to silent when I'm working. Less distracting that way." She picked up her purse and took her coat out of the closet. "I want to go visit my grandmother."

Don put on his stylish wool peacoat and held open the door. "After you."

Because it was so late in the afternoon, they hit traffic. It was dark by the time they arrived at Miller's Rest.

Not wanting to explain to Sadie why Don was following her around, she asked him to wait in the lobby. "I have your pager number. If I need you, I'll call."

"I'll escort you to your grandma's apartment," he said in a tone that left little doubt he wasn't going to back down.

"Fine," she conceded and led the way. At Sadie's door, she faced him. "Look. You can't stand out here in the hall. It'll upset the other residents and I really don't want to explain to Grams why you're here with me. So please, go back to the lobby."

His hard expression said he didn't like this. Too bad. She didn't want to upset her grandmother.

"You have my pager. Ring when you're ready to leave."

"I will," she said, glad he'd backed down.

"I mean it, Kristina. You don't leave this apartment without me."

She forced a smile past the anger creeping in. She hated being told what to do, but knew this was the only way to get what she wanted. She nodded her agreement.

She waited for Don to retreat back the way they came before knocking.

She heard a faint "come in."

Upon entering Sadie's apartment, Kris's gaze went directly to the bed where Sadie was sleeping. Again.

With a knot of worry in her chest, Kris addressed Gina. "Has she been sleeping long?"

"A few hours."

"Krissy?"

She rushed to her grandmother's side. Sadie smiled weakly, her breathing sounded forced.

"Grams, what's wrong? You don't sound good."

"I'm...not...sure," she managed to say.

"Here, let's sit you up." With Gina's help, Kris shifted Sadie to a more inclined position. Her breathing seemed to ease up.

"I feel so odd. Like all my muscles turned to jelly," Sadie described.

Kris exchanged a worried glance with Gina.

"She was fine earlier, and then said she needed to rest," Gina said. "I didn't realize that was abnormal."

"I'm getting the nurse." Kris hit the call button on the bed frame which would send a signal to the front desk that help was needed.

A few seconds later the door opened. A blonde nurse hurried in. "What's the problem?"

"Her breathing was very weak when I arrived. And she's very groggy. This isn't normal for her," Kris said, trying to keep anxiety from echoing in her voice.

"I'm Annie," the nurse introduced herself. She listened to Sadie's lungs and heart. "You're breathing is good now, Sadie. Was your chest feeling tight? Any sharp pain?"

Sadie shook her head. "No. Just jelly."

At Annie's questioning look, Kris explained, "She said her muscles felt like jelly."

A confused expression crossed Annie's face. "That is interesting. Have you taken any meds today besides your blood pressure medicine?"

Sadie shook her head.

"Any herbs?"

"Just some lemongrass tea."

"Well, that wouldn't account for relaxed muscles." Annie hung her stethoscope around her neck. "I'll ask Doc Crowley to come see you."

"Thank you," Kris said as the nurse left. Turning her attention to her grandmother, she asked, "You said you had some tea. With Mrs. Tipple?"

"Yes, dear. With Evelyn, Vivian and Ruth." A twinkle entered her eyes. "And Gabe stopped by. He's such a nice young man. You really ought to snag him before someone else does."

Kris straightened the bedcovers, keeping her face turned slightly away so her grandmother wouldn't see how her words affected her. "Grams, I've already told you. We're just friends."

Though she wished it were more. But wishing wasn't going to make it so. The only thing she knew that could make a difference was prayer. And she'd already told God what was on her heart. There really wasn't more for her to do, was there?

Pushing the subject from her mind, she thought about Mrs. Tipple's tea. The other day Kris had become ill after drinking Mrs. Tipple's lemongrass tea.

Her heart rate picked up speed. And she was sure that Sadie had mentioned that at least one of the missing people had also had tea with Mrs. Tipple. "Grams, do you remember if Carl or Lena or Denise had some of Mrs. Tipple's lemongrass tea before they went away?"

"Hmm. I do believe so. But it was such a long time ago now."

Kris started and exchanged a glance with Gina. Long time? It hadn't even been a full week since Sadie had insisted that her friends had gone missing. And since that point, Kris had reconnected with Gabe, her apartment door had been defaced, her tires slashed and someone had shot at her, hitting Gabe instead, and a van had tried to run her off the road. She shuddered at how close he'd come to serious injury.

"Cold?" Sadie asked.

"No. You?"

"A bit. I think I'll have dinner in here tonight."

Okay, Grams must really not feel well to willingly miss eating in the dining hall, which was usually one of Sadie's favorite parts of the day. A time when she could socialize before heading to the common room for board games.

"I'll go order your meal," Kris offered, glad for the excuse to leave the apartment because somehow she had to get a sample of Mrs. Tipple's teas. But how?

"I can get it," Gina offered.

"I'd rather you stayed with Sadie," Kris stated as she moved toward the door.

Kris took the long way to the dining hall so she wouldn't have to walk by Don. The last thing she needed was her shadow chasing after her. And she was thankful Gina had stayed put. Obviously she hadn't received the "don't let Kris out of your sight" memo.

Kris placed Sadie's dinner order, which she could

have easily phoned in as the attendant reminded her after promising to deliver the meal within the hour.

She then made her way through the independent living wing and paused in front of Mrs. Tipple's apartment. She pressed her ear to the molded, fiberglass door and listened, but heard no sound or movement from the other side.

Gathering her courage—Gabe was going to be so mad at her—she knocked, intending to tell Mrs. Tipple that she'd enjoyed the tea so much the other day that she'd like to take some home. It could work.

Her knock wasn't answered. She knocked louder.

A whisper of movement behind her sent her heart slamming against her ribs. She whirled around and found herself staring into Frank's dark, wary eyes.

A scream lodged in her throat.

TWELVE

Kris stifled her scream and stepped back until her shoulder blades pressed flat against the door. Frank looked as scared as she felt when he scurried around the other side of his cart. Why?

"What are you doing?" he asked, his gaze skittering away and back again. He held on to his cart like he was afraid it would take off without him. He wore his usual uniform and his face needed a shave. "You shouldn't be out roaming the halls."

"I was just coming to see Mrs. Tipple," Kris said, her voice sounding a bit reedy.

"She's in the common room." His glare darted down the hall toward the window and back again. "You need to leave." He rounded his shoulders and seemed to fold in on himself. "It's not safe."

"What?" She pushed away from the door. "Why isn't it safe?"

His shoulders hunched even more, deepening the impression that he wanted to hide within himself. He glanced once more down the hall toward the big picture window that showcased the courtyard now invisible in the night. "It's dark outside. Bad things happen in the dark."

"What? Tell me. What things?" she pressed.

He scrambled back a step, swinging his cart around. It bounced off the wall before straightening. He pushed the cart forward and practically ran away.

"Wait!" Kris started to follow him. He knew something. Something bad.

"Be careful," he said over his shoulder before hurrying around the corner and disappearing out of sight.

Hmph. Lot of help that was. He'd freaked her out.

She sighed, trying to slow her pulse. Well, she wasn't going to get any tea samples right now. She'd have to come back later.

Unless…she tried the doorknob. It turned easily in her hand. Mrs. Tipple really should learn to lock her apartment.

Stealthily, she entered and quickly shut the door behind her. Moving rapidly, she headed straight to the cupboard where Mrs. Tipple kept her teas. Taking four napkins from the holder, she spread them flat on the table and then put a scoop from each of the four loose tea jars on a napkin, then folded the napkin and tucked the samples into her pockets. She tidied up, making sure there was no evidence she'd been in the apartment.

At the door, she halted. What if it wasn't the tea leaves but something she puts in the tea after she made it?

She rushed back to the cupboards and swiftly began to search the kitchen, even though she had no idea what she was looking for. A bottle with the word *POISON* printed across the top would be helpful. But not likely.

She did find several clear liquid vials in the refrigerator. The plastic shrink wrap on the bottles read *Insulin*. A couple of the small containers had what appeared to be a splash of pink nail polish on the side as if Mrs. Tipple reached in with wet nails.

Shutting the fridge, Kris moved to the drawers. By the sink, she found Mrs. Tipple's junk drawer full of menus, bills, several bottles of eyedrops, mints, pens and miscellaneous stuff that was shoved in when one wasn't sure what to do with it. Kris had her own junk drawer. Well, actually, she had two.

There didn't seem to be anything overtly suspicious. Feeling like her time was running out, she abandoned her search and hastily left. She was out of breath by the time she reached Sadie's apartment.

Taking her cell phone, she ducked into the bathroom and called Gabe's cell.

"Burke."

"It's me, Kris."

"You okay?"

The slight lift of worry in his voice made her smile. "Yes, I'm fine. But I think I know what's going on."

"You do?"

She couldn't keep the excitement from her voice. "Yes. Mrs. Tipple is poisoning people."

There was as slight pause. "Mrs. Tipple?"

The disbelief in his tone was understandable. Mrs. Tipple seemed like such a nice, genteel woman. And Kris hadn't found anything concrete to support her theory. But still… "I know it sounds crazy, but listen to me. Carl, Lena, Denise. They all had tea not long before they went missing. I got sick right after drinking some of her tea. I think she's putting something in the teas she uses."

"Kris—"

"Think about it. You said you saw Grams drinking tea with her and now Grams isn't feeling well."

Kris took the silence as a good thing. At least she'd got his attention. "I got some samples of the teas."

"What? How? Where are you?" he yelled.

She held the phone away from her ear. She'd been right. He was mad. "I'm in Grams's room. I—" The words *snuck into her apartment* stuck in her throat.

"Go home. Right now."

His authoritative tone raised her hackles. She could just imagine the hard line of his jaw and the glitter of anger in his gem-colored eyes. "But what about the samples?"

"I'll come pick them up later. I'm going to text Donavan. You be ready to leave when he gets there."

She sighed. Better not to argue now. She wanted these samples tested.

Then he'd see that she was right.

Gabe snapped his cell phone closed. "She's going to be the death of me yet. I just know it." He then sent a text to Donavan asking him to please escort Kris to her parents' home ASAP.

"Oh?" Angie didn't even look away from her computer. "What's up?"

He ran a hand down his face, fatigue making his eyes burn and stress making his neck muscles tense. He tried to roll out the tension. "She's got it in her head that one of the little old ladies is poisoning people at the retirement center."

"Interesting. Does she have proof?"

He blew out a breath. "She has samples of teas."

His gaze fell to the open file folder in front of him. Had Mrs. Palmer drunk tea before her death? From what they'd gathered during their initial interview, Mrs. Palmer had eaten dinner in the cafeteria and retired early.

Ever since he'd returned to the station house, he'd been going back over the files of the three missing people and Debra Palmer, hoping to find something concrete to link the four.

He dug through the folders until he found the one with Mrs. Evelyn Tipple on the tab. He read through the file. She arrived in the states from London, England, twenty years earlier, married to a Jonathan Tipple and they'd lived just outside Boston in the small village of Hopkins. Husband died five years earlier and she'd taken up residence in Miller's Rest only three months ago. Nothing troublesome there.

"Sweet. We got a BOLO hit!"

Angie's excited voice drew Gabe's attention. "On the van?"

"Yep." She read from the screen. "Best of all, it was spotted near Miller's Rest."

Gabe snapped upright in his chair. "Where exactly?"

"A uniform saw the van parked outside of a mortuary. 'Curiousier and curiousier,'" she mused, rocking back in her chair. "It's registered as a company vehicle."

A chill skated across Gabe's neck. "What company?"

"Plank's Mortuary."

The residents' files forgotten, Gabe bolted to his feet. "Let's go."

"Wait." Her fingers flew over the keyboard. "Let me see who owns the place."

Impatiently, he took his sidearm out of the lockbox and slipped the weapon into his shoulder holster before shrugging into his overcoat, careful not to jostle his wounded arm.

"The owner is one Henry Hayes, mortician. I'm sending his name to NLETS."

Gabe stilled. "Hayes? As in Frank Hayes, the janitor at Miller's Rest?"

Angie lifted her gaze to meet his. "Brothers? Cousins?"

"It's a small world, but…"

"Not that small," she finished for him with a nod.

"Interesting," Gabe employed Angie's favorite word.

He thought back to Ms. Faust's anxiousness to have Mrs. Palmer's body sent to the mortuary. Plank's Mortuary? He grabbed the phone and dialed Miller's Rest Retirement Center.

When the receptionist answered, he identified himself, then asked, "What mortuary does the center use for their deceased patients?"

The receptionist didn't hesitate answering. "I believe it depends on what arrangements each individual has made prior to their death. Though I do know Ms. Faust has a working relationship with the owner of Plank's Mortuary. They're located just on the other side of the center's property line. Nice and handy. She has recommended them to several of our residents."

Exactly how nice and handy? he wondered. "Thank

you. You've been a big help," he said and hung up then filled Angie in.

"This is too much of a coincidence for it to be a coincidence."

"You think the retirement center's director and the local mortician are…what?"

Stumped as to why or even how the two could get rid of three people, he shook his head. "I don't know, but I intend to find out."

The phone on Angie's desk rang.

"Carlucci." She listened for a moment, then said, "We'll be right there." To Gabe she said, "The ME found something."

Kris heard the doorbell from her room on the second floor of her parents' home. She flew down the stairs and skidded to a halt at the sight of Gabe in the entryway talking with her father.

Gabe slid off his overcoat, revealing his dark suit, white shirt and a muted blue striped tie. She could just barely make out the bandage around his upper arm beneath the jacket.

Carrying the brown paper bag in which she'd deposited the tea samples, Kris descended the stairs. He hung his coat on the rack by the door and turned toward her with a slight smile that made her heart jump, and she smiled in return.

Her father said, "Kris, Gabe was just telling me the police might have a lead on the people who tried to run you off the road." He gestured them into the living room, where they found her mother and Don already settled.

Pleased, she looked at Gabe. "Really?"

He nodded. "We found the van you'd described. It belongs to the mortuary next door to Miller's Rest. We just have to figure out if the owner or one of the employees was driving the van at the time it tried to run you off the road. The owner, as it turns out, is Frank's brother. We also are having them brought in for questioning."

She raised her eyebrows. "Frank's brother owns the mortuary? That's odd, don't you think?"

"Very."

Her mother asked, "Who's Frank?"

Kris quickly explained Frank and his connection to Miller's Rest.

"What about the person who shot at you?" her father asked Gabe.

He shook his head. "Nothing concrete. The state troopers found shell casings for a common ammo. CSI pulled the same caliber bullets from my SUV."

Kris shuddered at the reminder of how close they had come to death. "What about the missing residents?"

His expression turned grim. "Nothing yet. But the ME found a hypodermic puncture wound in Mrs. Palmer's neck. And the tox screen revealed a combination of drugs in her system. A lethal combination."

Excitement filled her at learning what could very well be a major key to solving this mystery. But this was real life and horror replaced everything else. She fingered the bag in her hands. "So you think the doctor gave Mrs. Palmer something that killed her?"

"Maybe. Remember there are two doctors filling the

staff physician's post at Miller's Rest. We are bringing them in for questioning, too. We're also looking into all the medical personnel."

"Then really you haven't solved anything yet," her mother said.

He shook his head. "Not on the missing residents but on Debra Palmer's death we're closer than we were."

"Did Mrs. Palmer have any of Mrs. Tipple's tea?" Kris asked.

"Not that anyone remembered."

Frustrated because she was sure the elderly woman was involved somehow, Kris held up the bag and said, "Then these are probably a waste of time."

"I'll take them to the lab and have them checked out anyway."

"What are those?" her father asked.

"Kris gathered some of Mrs. Tipple's tea samples," Gabe answered.

She was thankful he hadn't explained just how she'd gathered the teas. He may have been mad at her method but he still respected her enough to take the samples. She appreciated that.

His fingers brushed against hers when he took the bag, reminding her of his touch, his kiss. She lifted her gaze to his. The light in his intense gaze made her wonder if he, too, was thinking about their brief special moments together.

He cleared his throat. "May I talk to you in private?"

There wasn't anything she wanted more. "Excuse us," she said as she grabbed Gabe by the sleeve and led him from the living room to her father's study.

As soon as the door closed behind them, he pulled her into his embrace. "Do you know how much you scared me today?"

"I did?" Her heart beat so hard she was sure he could feel the pounding rhythm through the fabric of her sweater and his suit.

"You can't keep doing stuff that puts you in needless danger."

Trying to downplay how much his concern pleased her, she replied quietly, "I didn't know you cared so much."

He ran a finger down her cheek. "Of course I care."

A shimmer of yearning touched her heart. "But just because it's your job, right?"

Some emotion she couldn't identify flashed across his face before he let her go and stepped back. She shouldn't have pushed. Regret knocked at her soul.

"Promise me that you'll be more careful and not do things like this." He held up the brown paper bag.

"I can't make you that promise," she said, wishing he'd take her back into his arms. But she was a job to him. He couldn't make her the kind of promises she needed to hear. What a pair they made.

He scoffed. "Of course not. Doing so would require actually following someone else's rule."

She narrowed her gaze. "What does that mean?"

Concern and determination battled in his eyes. "You have a bodyguard for a reason, Kris. Someone has tried to hurt you—"

His voice thickened with emotions. Maybe there was still hope.

He cleared his throat before speaking again. "Donavan is to accompany you wherever you go. Don't ditch him again."

A wave of annoyance rose, heating her cheeks. The familiar need to rebel nearly strangled her, but it was her recognizing it that took her by surprise. This was exactly how she felt every time her parents went autocratic on her.

Self-realization was a pain, she decided. Okay, she had a problem with authority. Something else to add to her prayer list.

"Please."

She almost didn't hear the note of pleading in his tone. Her irritation left in a swoosh. Gabe didn't deserve her anger, only her respect. "I won't."

"Good." The relief in his voice smoothed over her like a warming balm. He moved to the door and paused with his hand on the knob. "I'll let you know when we have more information."

She was too afraid that if she spoke she'd tell him of the feelings deep in her soul. So instead, she acknowledged Gabe's words by inclining her head.

As soon as he left the room, she sank into a leather chair. She could hear her parents talking with Don in the living room. Then she heard the audible click of the front door closing.

Lord, help me. I still have a long way to go to becoming the woman You'd have me be. But more than anything, can You please help me with my feelings for Gabe?

Because she'd made a mistake.

She'd fallen in love with him all over again.

* * *

"Hey, the chief wants to know why we have every holding room filled."

Gabe grimaced at his partner. Sunday mornings were usually pretty quiet around the station house. But today not so much.

First thing he'd done when he arrived at the station after arranging for use of the interrogation rooms was to call and check on Kris, only to find she'd gone to church and then to visit her grandmother.

A good thing actually. Because Gabe had had both Dr. Crowley and Dr. Sheffield from Miller's Rest brought in for questioning, as well as Ms. Faust, Frank Hayes and his brother Henry, the mortician, today of all days was a good day for Kris to be with Sadie.

So far Gabe's interrogations hadn't led anywhere. Both doctors had rock-solid alibis for the time surrounding Mrs. Palmer's death. And though Ms. Faust and the Hayes brothers had alibis, there were enough holes to make Gabe's gut queasy. "Yeah, well, tell the chief we're conducting an investigation."

Angie snorted. "You tell him yourself." She took a seat at her desk and grabbed a handful of files from the box sitting on the floor next to her feet. She was working through the Miller's Rest files, checking IDs against the NLETS since their initial pass through hadn't shed any light on the missing residents or Debra Palmer's death. "How's it going anyway?"

Gabe picked up a pencil and tapped it against the arm of his desk chair. "Not as productive as I'd hoped. I have to let the doctors go soon. As for the other three…"

He paused, remembering the cagey way Henry Hayes had acted.

The man was hiding something. Hayes claimed he was not at the wheel of the van that had tried to run Kris off the road. Though he owned the vehicle and his prints—along with all of his employees—were found in the van, there was no proof one of the other mortuary staff hadn't been driving at the time. Only none of the three staff members had any connection to Miller's Rest.

The intersection cameras by Kris's apartment hadn't revealed a thing. Whoever was driving had known how to avoid being seen.

And then there was Ms. Faust who, much to Gabe's chagrin, asked for a lawyer the moment she reached the station, which shut down any questioning. That hadn't instilled much confidence in her innocence but what exactly had she done? And why?

That left Frank.

But Gabe didn't think Frank had the brains or the courage to kill anyone. The man nearly fainted when Gabe raised his voice. A stone-cold killer Frank was not. But an accomplice?

"Hey, Burke." Crime Scene Technician Carlos Perez approached Gabe's desk. His white lab coat hung open, revealing the wild print shirt beneath.

Gabe held up a hand, pretending to be blinded by the sight. "Whoa, Carlos, that shirt. Really, dude."

Carlos grinned, showing teeth a bit too big for his mouth. "You no like? Come on, dude, this is an authentic Tijuana shirt. Straight from the streets."

Gabe rolled his eyes. "You didn't come up here to blind me."

"No, I didn't. Two of those tea samples you sent down had traces of tetrahydrozoline HCL," Carlos said.

"Really?"

Angie abandoned the file she'd just opened. "Wow, your girlfriend was right," she said, clearly impressed.

"Yeah." Gabe didn't correct Angie's assumption about Kris being his girlfriend. He rather liked the sound of it. Liked the idea of taking that next step. He should have had more faith in Kris's instincts. *Mrs. Tipple had been poisoning the residents.* Go figure. "Tetra—what is it?"

"A common substance found in eyedrops. Used in the eyes, it's fine, gets the red out no problem, but ingested it can be deadly. At the very least, brings on a violent bout of nausea and lowers blood pressure and body temp, and makes breathing difficult," Carlos explained.

Oh, no. All the symptoms Kris displayed when she'd been sick. Both Kris and Sadie had had the contaminated tea. A shudder of horror ripped through Gabe. Kris could have died. He had to stop Mrs. Tipple.

"Hey, wasn't that one of the substances found in Mrs. Palmer's tox screen?" Angie asked.

Gabe searched through the papers lying haphazardly on his desk until he found the ME's report on Mrs. Palmer.

Sure enough, one of the two substances found in Debra Palmer's blood was tetrahydrozoline HCL. Obviously, Mrs. Palmer had drunk some tea. "Yes. The other was a sedative used mainly in surgery called succinylcholine. But how did Mrs. Tipple acquire that prescription drug?"

"Good question," Carlos said. "I'll leave you to answer it."

"Thanks, Carlos. You're the bomb." Gabe grabbed the phone and called the dispatcher requesting a patrol car to pick up Mrs. Evelyn Tipple for questioning. Then he called Miller's Rest and asked for Sadie's room. Kris answered, her voice a welcome sound.

"You were right, Kris. Mrs. Tipple was putting poison in her teas. I'm having her brought in for questioning."

"Oh, Gabe! Do you think she is behind the disappearances? And how could she find someone to shoot at us? Along with the other attempts on my life?"

Her rapid-fire questions made him want to smile despite the very unpleasant situation. Kris just did that to him. She made the wrong right. She made him care about a whole bunch of stuff he never gave a thought to before. Her and Sadie. He was so glad he could keep them safe. "I'll find out when I question Mrs. Tipple."

"Thanks for letting me know. I don't think I'll mention this…"

"Understandable," Gabe said, liking how considerate Kris was of her grandmother's feelings. Mrs. Tipple was undoubtedly a big part of Sadie's life, and to think the woman wanted to kill her was rotten. He couldn't imagine what motivated the elderly woman.

"I guess your job is almost done." There was a strange hitch in her voice.

A funny ache started in his chest. What excuse would he use to see her once this was over? "Yeah, almost. There are still unanswered questions though. So don't relax too much."

"I won't. Goodbye."

"Bye." Gabe slowly put the handset down, wondering at the wistful note in her voice. Was she growing to care for him again? Did he dare hope so? And if so, then what? He cared for her, but was it enough? He thought back to the jealousy he felt when Kris had been talking so closely to Don. Did that mean he was in love with her? All the times he'd held her, the time they had kissed and all the many ways she had touched his soul rose to the forefront of his mind. Was he in love?

Around him phones rang and people went about their daily routine as his world, as he knew it, was suddenly spinning in a new direction.

"Hey, Mr. Daydreamer." Angie's voice broke through his thoughts.

Forcing his mind to the task at hand, he rose. "I'm going to take another run at the doctors. One of them had to supply Mrs. Tipple with the sedative."

She held up her hand. "Question—you think this old woman was the one who shot at you and tried to run down Kris with the mortuary van?"

He blew out a breath of aggravation. "My gut's telling me no way. My guess, Henry Hayes, but why, I don't know." No, Gabe's job was definitely not done. "Let's solve one mystery at a time, okay?"

"I'll let you know when the little old lady arrives," Angie said, turning back to her computer and the files stacked in front of her.

Gabe headed into the first interrogation room where Dr. Crowley sat at the metal table.

"Can I leave?" Crowley asked as Gabe walked in.

"Just a few more questions," Gabe replied as he took a seat opposite the doctor. "Tell me about your relationship with Mrs. Evelyn Tipple."

Confusion entered Crowley's gaze. "Evelyn? She's a resident. I've had limited contact with her. Why?"

"Any idea how she'd come by succinylcholine?"

Crowley's eyes widened. "Excuse me? We don't keep that on hand. Why would she have a sedative like that?"

Holding on to his patience, Gabe said, "That's what I'm trying to find out. If you didn't supply her with the drug, then who did?"

Crowley shrugged. "We don't stock succinylcholine."

"What about Dr. Sheffield?"

"No. He would never—" Crowley halted. "At least I don't think he would. I've known John for twenty years. He's a good man."

"We'll see if he says the same about you." Gabe rose and left the room. He headed toward the interrogation room at the end of the hall. Angie came running up, waving a piece of paper in the air.

"Gabe, you'll never believe this," Angie said as she skidded to a halt.

With a dry snort, Gabe said, "Let me guess, Mrs. Tipple's identification was forged."

Angie shook her head. "No." She held out the paper for his perusal.

He blinked in disbelief as he read about a woman wanted in Arizona for the murder of several nursing home victims under her care. He stared at the picture on the warrant.

How had he missed her?

He fumbled for his cell phone and speed-dialed Kris. The call went straight to voice mail. He rang Donavan.

"Cavanaugh."

"Where are you?" Gabe asked.

"Specifically? In the men's room at Miller's Rest. I've got the flu or something."

Fear gripped Gabe's insides in a choke hold. "Where's Kris?"

"With her grandmother. Gina—" Donavan retched in Gabe's ear. "Sorry about that."

"Gina? Is what?" he barked as panic boiled in his blood.

"She's sick, too. A nurse took her to the infirmary."

He hung up and dialed Miller's Rest. The receptionist put him through to Sadie's room. There was no answer.

If ever there was a time Gabe needed to put his faith in someone other than himself, that time was now.

Please, God in Heaven, if You really do love me as Kris claims, please, don't let any harm come to her! I need her.

Please let them be in the common room or the dining hall. Anywhere safe.

His heart rammed against his ribs, demanding to be heard, but he couldn't go there, not now when Kris was in danger.

Because Kris wouldn't know *not* to trust Vivian Kirk, aka Veronica Krauss, registered nurse and murderer.

"We've got to get to the center!" He ran from the station with Angie on his heels.

THIRTEEN

Knowing she'd been right about Mrs. Tipple didn't make Kris feel good. Why would the elderly lady, who seemed so sweet and generous, want to hurt others? But one could never tell what was in another person's heart. Only God could look deep inside and comprehend the motivations which drove someone to kill.

Or deny love as Gabe had done.

Her heart twisted with anguish for what he was missing in his life. What they were missing together. She couldn't imagine a life without love. It would be so empty.

With a sigh, Kris sent the rocker moving with the toe of her shoe. The soft sound of friction between the wooden slats gliding back and forth against the carpet in Sadie's apartment was soothing, especially mixed with the low Christmas music coming from the CD player. A reminder that the holiday was fast approaching. And she wasn't ready. Neither was Sadie.

With so much upheaval in their lives, Kris hadn't had a moment to take Sadie shopping. Last year they'd hounded the holiday bazaars at several local churches, finding unique presents for their small family unit. This year…nothing.

Kris worried her bottom lip as she stared at her resting grandmother. Anxiety painfully tightened her shoulders. Sadie wasn't getting any better. Maybe Mrs. Tipple's tea wasn't the culprit.

According to Gina, Dr. Crowley had come to visit Sadie yesterday and had ordered some blood tests. They hadn't received the results yet and waiting for them was torturing Kris. She needed answers.

Kris glanced at the clock on the wall. Gina should have returned by now with Sadie's lunch. Not that Sadie was awake to eat yet. But Kris was hopeful that getting some food in her stomach when she woke up would revive her physically, since Gina had said Sadie hadn't any appetite the night before.

Self-reprisal crunched through Kris. She should have been here to take care of Sadie. Instead, she'd moped about her parents' house, silently bemoaning the fact she'd fallen in love with Gabe again.

Would she ever learn from her mistakes?

The man was all wrong for her on so many levels. Cynical about love, skeptical about God and married to his job. Not good. Not good at all.

She bowed her head and silently sent up prayers of understanding and acceptance of her feelings for Gabe. She really had no other choice than to acknowledge the reality of the situation and learn to live with the loss. Again. She was sure once this crisis was over, that would be it. He'd walk back out of her life. Sadness and regret pinched her heart at the loss of what wouldn't be. What Gabe wouldn't allow in his life. Her love.

She said a prayer of healing for Sadie, asking for the doctor to be given wisdom on treating her grandmother.

And she said a prayer of salvation and forgiveness for Mrs. Tipple.

The sound of the apartment door opening brought Kris's prayers to a halt. She lifted her gaze, expecting to see Gina arriving with a tray of food. Surprise filled Kris as Vivian Kirk shut the door with a click and ambled in, her round face alight with a good-natured smile. Her graying, blond hair curled in disarray around her head and the oversized cardigan sweater added to her ample figure.

Did the woman know how to knock? It was one thing for her to enter her friend Evelyn's apartment unannounced but to do that to Sadie's was odd and rude. Kris forced a smile. Obviously the older woman was a bit off. "Mrs. Kirk? What are you doing here?"

"Oh, please, call me Vivian." She toddled farther into the room, her tennis shoes making no noise against the carpet. "I just saw Sadie's new full-time guard in the dining hall. She told me you were here. I thought I'd come say hello."

"That was thoughtful," Kris said, uneasy that apparently it was common knowledge that Gina wasn't just a nurse.

"How is Sadie today?"

"Still under the weather."

"Yes, she does look a bit peaked, doesn't she?"

Kris murmured her agreement.

"Your grandmother is lucky to have someone to care for her. Some of us aren't so lucky. Some of us could disappear and no one would care or even notice."

The seriously ominous words caught Kris off guard, but then she realized there was such a sad note in Vivian's voice. Kris's chest ached with compassion and her mind immediately jumped to the three missing residents. "That's not true. People do notice and care."

Something flickered in Vivian's light brown eyes. "You're right, of course. Inquisitive people everywhere."

A bit put off by that odd comment, Kris asked, "You don't have any family close by?"

"It's always been me against the world."

There was a slight note of defensive anger in the older woman's tone that confused Kris. "I'm so sorry."

She patted Kris's arm and smiled indulgently. "Don't feel sorry for me. I have a purpose." She stepped closer to the bed. "What keeps you busy when you're not here tending to your grandmother?"

"I'm a photographer by trade."

"Oh, how exciting. You must tell me more." Vivian sat on the edge of Sadie's bed.

Kris thought it odd Vivian would take such a liberty, but shrugged the behavior off as that of an eccentric woman. And obviously since Sadie was still sound asleep, Vivian's presence wasn't bothersome. "I have a studio downtown," Kris explained. "I do mostly advertising work but for a few months each year I travel to various missionary outposts and take pictures for the ministries. It helps to show people the fruit of their labor."

"That is very philanthropic of you. Your parents must be so proud."

Not wanting to get into her family dynamics, Kris made a noncommittal noise. She hadn't really thought of her work with the various ministries as philanthropic. That was a label she placed on her parents' endeavors. They gave of their monetary resources and encouraged others to do the same, while Kris gave of her time and equipment to encourage others to give. Was either form of charity better or worse?

Could it be she and her parents weren't so very different after all? The realization was a heavy one especially after the revelations of her misconstrued ideas of their relationship with Sadie from a few days ago. Her perceptions of her parents kept changing. And she truly liked what she was seeing. Go figure.

"I don't see your parents here often."

Vivian's comment brought Kris's mind back to the conversation. "Their visits were too upsetting for Sadie. Ms. Faust thought it best they not visit often."

Vivian's gaze wandered toward the window. "Ah, yes, Cynthia does take direction well," Vivian murmured.

Kris frowned. *"What?"*

Vivian brought her gaze back to Kris and raised her eyebrows in question. "What? I'm sorry. I was lost in thought."

"You said something about Cynthia? Who's Cynthia?"

"Did I?" Vivian shrugged. "Silly me." She leaned in closer in a conspiratorial way. "Did you know that a police officer took Mrs. Tipple away?"

Kris smoothed her hand over the wooden arm of the

rocker. She should feel safe with Evelyn Tipple in custody but anxious little butterflies still fluttered in her gut. "Yes, I'd heard."

"Do you know why?" Vivian stared at her with wide bloodshot eyes.

"Um…I'm sure the police have their reasons," Kris said, unwilling to get into the specifics. She didn't want to upset Vivian.

A smug smile spread over Vivian's round face as she straightened. "She did bad things. She made people sick with her tea."

Kris blinked. "You know?"

A dry chuckle turned into a slight cough. Vivian cleared her throat and then said, "Oh, yes. But she doesn't."

Kris drew her eyebrows together in confusion. "She doesn't?"

"No." Glee lit up her expression. "But she'll be arrested and put in jail just the same. I have it all worked out. The police are so easy to manipulate."

Shocked by the words so incongruent with the genial woman, Kris vaulted to her feet. "I don't understand." A slithering of apprehension galvanized Kris to stand protectively beside Sadie. "What have you *worked out?*"

Vivian slid from the bed and crowded closer to Kris. "You see, dear, it's questions like yours that get you in trouble. You should have listened to my first warning."

Shock sent a tremor cascading down Kris's spine as the meaning of the words solidified in her mind. "You defaced my apartment door?"

Vivian casually put her hands into the pockets of her bulky sweater. She rocked back on the heels of her tennis shoes. "I did. I had hoped you would do as you were told." She shook her head sadly. "But no. You just kept pushing, didn't you? Had to involve the police. Just had to go searching for Denise. What a nuisance you've been."

Her mind reeling with the implications of what she was hearing, Kris's hand sought the call button on the bed while she tried to distract Vivian by keeping her talking. "You did something to Carl, Lena and Denise. Where are they?"

Vivian's now razor-sharp gaze pierced through Kris. The physical change in her demeanor was as unsettling as her words. "That won't help you. I've already disabled the alarm."

Swallowing back her rising fear, Kris considered bolting for help, but fear for Sadie kept her feet in place. "How? When?"

She smiled serenely. "Everything is *plug and play* these days, so high-tech around here. And I came in last night when I brought your grandmother some delicious pudding."

Rage roared as thunderous as a train through Kris's mind, pushing back the fear. "Is that why she's sick? Did you lace the pudding with something?"

"Oh, you are a smart one, aren't you? Yes, I used the same ingredient to taint Evelyn's teas."

Infuriated, Kris demanded, "How could you do this! Why?"

"It needed to be done."

Vivian's expression showed no remorse; instead her benevolent smile made Kris shudder. The woman was clearly deranged. Kris's gaze searched the room for her purse with her cell phone. Crud! It was over by the sink. She couldn't risk moving from her place beside her grandmother. Who knew what Vivian would do? Kris stole a glance at the door. Where was Gina?

Vivian chuckled, the sound ripping along Kris's flesh like the thorn of a sticker bush. "I can see what you're thinking. But your friend Gina won't be returning. She was taken to the infirmary and I would hazard a guess that the man who's been guarding you is there by now, as well."

A rocket of horror launched in the pit of Kris's stomach. "What did you do to them?"

"Well, to your young man, I acted the gracious host and gave him a big cup of coffee. He did look like he was fighting to stay awake in the lobby. And Gina, well, she was a little harder to convince. But she took the hot chocolate I offered, I think mainly to get me to shut up." Vivian giggled. "I just love when my plans come together."

Kris's gaze landed on the bedside phone. Unfortunately it was on the other side of Sadie. If she worked her way around the bed, then she could at least knock the receiver off. The receptionist would figure something was wrong when the light continually flashed at the front desk, right?

Vivian followed her gaze. "Uh-oh. No, no." She wagged a finger. "Don't even think about it. You'll have to get by me to reach the phone. And that's not going to happen."

Kris's gaze narrowed on the other woman. Kris could take her down in a heartbeat. But her mind worked to formulate a less violent plan. Keep her talking. Some-

one had to check on Sadie at some point. Besides, surely
Gina or Don would let Gabe know they were sick and
he'd come here. She sent up a prayer for help. She really
didn't want to have to hurt Vivian.

Gently taking Sadie's hand in her own, Kris drew
strength from her love. Sadie stirred but didn't wake.
"You didn't answer me. What did you do with Carl,
Lena and Denise? Where are they?" Kris imagined them
trapped in some dark room, wasting away. She shuddered at the image.

"Dead," Vivian stated simply, her voice holding not
a trace of regret. "Cremated, actually."

Gabe's words about the mortuary rang in Kris's head.
The van that had tried to run her off the road belonged to
the mortuary. She swallowed back the bile that rose in her
throat. Anger pounded at her temples. "How could you?"

"Oh, it was quite easy, really. Of course I did have
some help. I don't get around like I used to."

Thinking of Sadie's suspicions that Ms. Faust was up
to no good, Kris asked, "Is Ms. Faust aware of what
you're up to?"

Vivian face twisted in confusion. "Of course. Didn't
I already say that?"

Kris blinked. No. "Why would she agree to this
madness?"

"As I said, Cynthia Faust follows direction well, though
she wasn't on board at first. It took some fancy talking on
Henry's part to convince her, but eventually, Cynthia saw
the wisdom in relieving these poor souls of the burdens
they carried." She let out a small chuckle. "Besides, she
liked cashing their checks and pocketing the money."

"Burdens? Who's Henry? She did this for money?" Kris had never faced evil before and had certainly never expected it to come from someone like Vivian, who appeared like such a nice motherly type.

"Henry's my son."

The words barely registered. Kris's gaze was riveted to the hypodermic needle Vivian pulled out of her sweater pocket. Alarm swamped Kris in a violent wave. "What are you planning to do?"

"Rid myself of you. You've made me very angry. I don't like to be angry. It's not pleasant."

The words were delivered with a congenial smile as if she were talking about something mundane rather than about something as insane as murder. Kris's muscles tensed. Every fiber of her being screamed attack before Vivian could do anything. Mentally, Kris picked out the other woman's vulnerable spots—eyes, throat, knees, instep.

"Krissy?"

Kris jumped in surprise at the sound of her grandmother's reedy voice. Sadie stared up at Kris, her cloudy blue eyes full of confusion and fear.

Kris squeezed Sadie's arm. "Shh. It's going to be okay." *Oh, please, let it all be okay. God help us. Send Gabe.*

"Hmm, I didn't take you as a liar," Vivian said as she moved closer, trapping Kris against the bed railing.

Kris planted both hands on Vivian's chest and shoved. Vivian stumbled back a step. Keeping herself between the madwoman and her grandmother, Kris ground out, "I'm not a liar. God will protect us. You and your evil are not wanted here."

Vivian gave a short laugh. "Ha. Let's see how well He protects you from this." She raised the needle high and lunged toward Kris's neck.

Using both hands, Kris grabbed Vivian's wrist, and with every ounce of strength she possessed held her attacker at bay. But Vivian was strong, stronger than Kris would have imagined.

Enough of this! Kris rammed her knee into Vivian's stomach, but they were so close because of the bed, Kris's angle was off, making the blow less powerful. A swoosh of air left Vivian but she didn't relent. Instead, she seemed to gain strength, pushing forward. Kris kicked repeatedly, connecting with Vivian's shin. Unfazed, Vivian bared her teeth with a guttural growl.

Disbelief and fear clawed at Kris's mind. *Please, God.* Hanging on to Vivian's wrist, Kris bent backward, nearly lying atop Sadie.

"Oh, my. Oh, no. Help!" Sadie screamed, her weak voice barely carrying from the bed.

Taking her grandmother's cue, Kris began to scream while keeping her whole focus on the sharp tip of the needle held inches above her skin and moving ever closer.

She *so* did not want to die. There was still so much she had to do in her life, so much unsaid. She wanted to tell Gabe she loved him.

A woman's scream filled the hallway.

Gabe's heart slammed against his chest with terror as he raced toward Sadie's apartment. Not even taking the time to see if the lock had been engaged, he used his good shoulder as a ramming device, throwing all his weight against the door.

The lock did indeed pop and the door swung open. Gabe stumbled forward, quickly regained his balance and sucked in a terrified breath at the sight of Kris locked in a deadly battle for control of a syringe held in the tight grip of the shorter, elderly woman whose picture he'd just seen on a rap sheet.

Rage colored the world as he shot forward, his arms encircling Vivian Kirk in a bear hug. In a swift movement, he easily lifted the older woman off the floor and dumped her in the corner. Angie had stormed in right behind him and already had her cuffs out. Vivian greeted her with curses as Angie and an officer worked to subdue her.

"Krissy!" Sadie's weak cry instilled fear in Gabe's soul and brought his attention flying back around to see Kris sink to the floor. Were they too late? Had Kris been injected with a drug?

His heart cried out to God. *Please, no. Show me You love me. Don't let her die.*

Gabe dropped to his knees and gathered Kris in his arms. Her breathing was shallow and her pupils dilated with shock.

He searched her neck for a puncture wound with trembling fingers. Her delicate skin was unmarred. The needle hadn't made contact. Adrenaline drained from his veins and left him feeling light-headed. He hadn't been too late.

Around them the room became a buzz of activity as more law enforcement personnel arrived, taking Vivian away, and the retirement center's medical staff rushed in to care for Sadie. Nurse Annie checked Kris's vitals and confirmed that Kris was in shock but would be all right.

Relieved, Gabe smoothed back Kris's hair. "Kris, honey, you're okay. I'm here."

"Gabe?" Kris blinked, her gaze focusing on him. "Grams?"

"She's fine."

Kris stiffened. "Vivian!"

"Dealt with," he replied. "You don't have to worry about her anymore."

Kris's lip trembled. "The missing residents are dead. She killed them."

Though he'd suspected as much, the knowledge left a bitter taste. "She'll be going away for the rest of her life."

Kris clutched at his shirt. "She had help. Her son Henry and Ms. Faust."

Gabe blinked, stunned to learn that Henry was Vivian's son. And Frank, for that matter. Okay, that added another twist. One he'd sort out later. "Don't worry. Henry and Ms. Faust are in custody. You and Sadie are both safe now."

"What about Gina and Don? Are they okay? That woman poisoned them!"

Gabe had guessed that was the cause of both body-guards' and several nurses' sudden illnesses and had dispatched paramedics to the center while Angie drove him at a breakneck speed to Miller's Rest. "They're being cared for. Though Don was found crawling his way here from the men's room. He was trying to do his job, but…he's pretty sick."

Kris melted against him with a sigh of pure relief. "You're here. I prayed you'd come."

Tears burned the back of Gabe's eyes. He lifted her into his arms and carried her out of the chaotic room to a quiet alcove down the hall. "He answered both of our prayers."

She sat next to him on the couch. She stared at him, her clear blue eyes wide. "You prayed? For me?"

Tightening his hold on her, Gabe nodded. "I told Him if He really loved me, to show me by keeping you safe."

Her expression fell slightly. "You can't bargain with God. That's not true faith."

"Ah, but I'm a Doubting Thomas, remember? I needed a little visual aid to help in my faith."

She seemed to consider his words for a moment, then relaxed back against his chest. "You know Thomas went on to preach the gospel throughout the world."

Gabe kissed the top of her head. "Let's just take things one step at a time, okay? God and I have to get to know each other a bit first."

She snuggled closer and lifted her face. "I can live with that. And I have to tell you—" She tugged at her bottom lip with her teeth.

He smoothed back her hair. "What?"

"I love you."

Unexpected joy exploded in his chest. He opened his mouth to speak, to say…what? He didn't know. He clamped his lips tight. All the emotions he'd been holding back since he'd first met her eight years ago expanded, making his heart ache.

Something in his expression must have made her believe the worst, because she put her fingers to his lips.

"I know you don't believe in love and I'm not telling

you this to make you feel bad or guilty. I just… For a moment, I thought Vivian might win and I hadn't told you." A tear rolled down her cheek and dropped to soak into his shirt.

Gabe pulled her to his chest and held on tight. "You were scared. Everything's going to be all right now."

He wanted to tell this strong, spirited, brave and beautiful woman she was wrong, he *did* believe in love. She'd taught him that love was there all along, he just hadn't recognized it. But common sense told him that he should wait for a more appropriate time. Like next Saturday night when they went on their date.

He eased away from her. He had no other choice. If he didn't get moving, he'd give in to her inviting lips and kiss her. Not a good idea when there was so much that was still unresolved in their lives. "Is it okay if we talk about all of this later?"

She wrapped her arms around her middle and nodded.

He could only pray that love would be enough.

Kris paced the living room of her apartment waiting for Gabe to arrive for their date. It had been nearly a week since she'd seen him, though he had called several times to check on Sadie. And when he'd called earlier today, he wouldn't tell her where they were going, so she'd had to guess on the appropriate attire and went with soft tan cords and a lightweight rainbow-striped sweater. She'd pulled her hair back into a ponytail and applied a touch of mascara.

Maybe he hadn't told her what the plan was because there wasn't one.

She was sure her declaration of love had shocked him and probably built a higher wall between them. His promise to "talk about this" was probably nothing more than his segue to a royal rejection. A repeat of the past.

Taking deep cleansing breaths, she tried to keep her mind and heart from throbbing with conjecture. She'd taken a risk in telling him of her love. She had to be prepared for him to walk away again. Just as he had eight years ago. Only this time, she wouldn't regret loving him. He'd taught her so much about life and helped her to see her family in a new light. She'd do whatever it took, no matter how long or how hard it would be to make him see they belonged together.

Her heart would always belong to Gabe Burke.

Anticipation held back the exhaustion she should have been feeling. Sleep hadn't come easily since that fateful day when Vivian attacked her. And every day Kris had spent time with Sadie as the doctors worked to rid her body of the toxins Vivian had given her. Even Kris's parents had visited the center. Kris was relieved to confirm she'd misjudged her parents. There were so many layers to their relationship with Sadie that Kris had been unaware of. She supposed neither her parents nor Sadie had explained the many facets in an effort to protect her, from what she wasn't sure.

The knowledge was freeing in some ways, yet left Kris emotionally on new and unfamiliar ground. She felt like she was finally seeing her parents through adult eyes. Took her long enough.

She glanced at the clock. Just a few more minutes and Gabe would arrive. She couldn't wait to see him. He'd become such an important part of her life again. He'd saved her life.

And now her future hung in the balance. Nervous energy had her quickening her steps.

She jumped when the buzzer sounded. She depressed the intercom. "Yes?"

"It's Gabe."

Her heart rammed against her ribs as she pushed the button to let him into the building.

After taking a second to quickly check her appearance in the mirror on the wall, she opened the door.

Gabe strode down the hall toward her, looking handsome in jeans and a leather bomber. His jaw was cleanly shaven and his hair neatly combed back. But it was the sparkling light in his green eyes as he stopped in front of her that caused her pulse to leap. Could it be love? Or was that just wishful thinking?

"May I come in?" he asked.

Heat suffused her cheeks. She couldn't believe she was just standing there staring like a dummy without even greeting him. Her nerves were really getting to her. She stepped aside. "Hi. Of course, please, come in."

He crowded past her, sending her senses reeling with the clean, spicy scent of his aftershave. She noticed a garment bag hung from his fingers. She inclined her head toward the bag. "What do you have there?"

"We'll get to that," he said and laid the bag across the back of a chair before sitting on the couch. He held out his hand. "Come here."

She swallowed back rising trepidation. He wasn't going to waste any time rebuffing her love. She sat beside him, their knees touching, an achy kind of dread creeping over her.

He gathered her hands in his. "Let me bring you up to speed on everything. Vivian Kirk confessed to killing Carl Remming, Lena Street, Denise Jamesen and Debra Palmer."

Kris shuddered with the remembered fear of her struggle with Vivian. If not for Gabe, Kris could be dead right now. "She'd said she was relieving them of their burdens. Did she explain that?"

Gabe lifted a shoulder. "She's insane. She really believed she was helping them in some twisted way."

"What about her son?"

"Sons," he said. "Henry Hayes, the mortuary owner, is her son and so is Frank, the janitor."

Kris dropped her jaw. "Really?"

"Seems the boys' father took off with them when they were little. Vivian found her sons some years later after their father died and took custody of them. They were completely under her control. And it seems Ms. Faust and Henry were romantically involved."

"Why keep their relationship a secret?"

"It wouldn't look good for the retirement center director to recommend her boyfriend's mortuary to the residents."

"What a tangled, evil web those people wove."

He squeezed her hands. "But they wouldn't have been stopped if you hadn't cared enough to get involved. That took a lot of guts. I'm proud of you."

His praise sent warmth curling through her. "It was Sadie who really started the ball rolling."

"Very true. She's one special lady. Just like her granddaughter."

Inordinately pleased by the compliment, she smiled. "Thank you."

"I mean every word. You are special." He hesitated as if gathering his thoughts.

She braced herself, ready to counter any argument with why they belonged together.

Finally, he spoke. "One of the things I love about you is how willing you are to do the hard thing. To face your issues head-on. That's why I really think we should attend the fundraiser with your parents."

Her mind was stuck on that little four-letter word— *love*—he'd so causally dropped that the rest of what he said took a moment to register. When it did, she felt as if she'd been punched in the gut.

She jerked her hands away. "Attend—what? Are you kidding me?"

His mouth quirked at the corners. "You look as surprised as your mom did when I stopped by to ask if we could still come."

She raised both eyebrows. "My mom didn't put you up to this?"

"No. This is my idea." His expression implored her to listen. "Kris, you are a Worthington. Part of who you are will always be a Worthington no matter how much you try to deny the connection. And if there is ever to be a chance for us, we have to accept that part of you."

He swallowed and dropped his gaze for a second. When he lifted his eyes, the sincerity in the green depths tore at her. "*I* have to accept that part of you."

Her mind ping-ponged through the various statements he made and globbed on to the one that mattered to her the most. "A chance for us?" She couldn't breathe. She couldn't have heard him right. "You want there to be a chance for us?"

"I do." A tender smile touched his well-formed mouth. "I know I said I don't believe in love, but I was wrong. You made me recognize that love is real. That I can feel love. And I do. For you, Kris. I love you. You're the strongest spirited and bravest woman I've ever met. I can't believe how blessed I am to be given a second chance with you."

Tears of elation gathered in her eyes and delight tinged with relief bounced through her. God had answered her prayers more generously than she'd imagined. "I love you, too."

"I know." He pulled her to him and kissed her.

She melted, her whole being sinking into the sensations and emotions running through her system.

"Kris," he murmured against her lips.

"Hmm?"

"Will you attend the fundraiser with me?"

She broke away and stared at him as the rest of what he'd said finally filtered through her mind. "What did you mean 'you have to accept that part of me'? We don't have to live in my parents' world."

"Kris, you could no more cut your parents out of your life than you can Sadie. And you shouldn't want to. We need to honor your parents together."

The earnest love she saw etched in his handsome face made all the silly resistance that sprang to her mind drain away. He was right. Deep down she did love her parents and wanted to honor them.

Tonight she'd introduce her parents to the man she wished to one day marry. Hope abounded in her heart. "All right. I'll go." She eyed the garment bag. "Is that a tux?"

He grinned. "You know me so well. And something for you. Your mom told me your size."

Her eyes widened. "You bought me a dress? That's so romantic." The thought of her big, tough, wounded cop going dress shopping for her brought a fresh wave of delighted tears to her eyes. She leaned in for another kiss as contentment settled over her.

"Kris?"

"Hmm?"

He pulled away from her mouth to smile. "We better get going," he said and unzipped the garment bag. "I hope you like it. I think the color will match your eyes perfectly."

The unsure expression on his dear face filled her to overflowing with more and more love. "I'm sure I'll love the dress."

He took out the black tux. "I'll use your powder room to change and meet you out here in ten."

Excited by the prospect of their future, she jumped up and ran to her bedroom. She made a small "oh" sound as she took out the capped sleeved, cornflower-blue evening gown from the garment bag. The delicate fabric swished as she quickly changed into the dress.

She beamed with happiness as she gazed at her reflection in the mirror on her closet door. Beaded lace covered the bodice and veered to a point at the waist with the folds of the skirt draping becomingly to the floor.

She slipped her feet into a pair of navy heels before brushing out her hair, letting the length flow over her shoulders. Quickly she applied fresh lipstick and put on the pearl necklace and matching earrings that Sadie had given her for her twenty-first birthday.

Her ten minutes were up. She entered the living room to find Gabe waiting. She gave a sigh of pure feminine bliss as she gazed at the handsome picture he made in his tux with the Christmas tree lights twinkling behind him.

"Just a sec," she said and ran to her work studio. Grabbing the camera off her workbench, she returned to the living room snapping shots of Gabe.

With a laugh, he said, "Enough already." He held out his hand. "You are beyond beautiful," he murmured before bringing her hand to his lips.

"You are, too," she replied and allowed him to help her into her coat.

He paused with his hand on the doorknob. "We have one stop to make on the way."

"Oh?"

"Your parents asked me to invite my mother."

Joy that she'd finally meet his family filled her already-bursting heart. "That's awesome. What more surprises could this night hold?"

"One more," he said with a gleam in his eyes.

She liked this playful, fun side to him. "Do tell."

"Your parents are picking up Sadie, as well."

Kris's hand pressed over her heart. Tears of joy

gathered. She couldn't ask for a more perfect Christmas gift, sent directly from above.

Tonight was a night for family and love. A night full of light. No more chasing shadows.

* * * * *

Dear Reader,

The idea for this story came to me while I was visiting my maternal grandmother in an assisted living facility. I loved and respected my grandmother very much. I miss her greatly. She suffered with dementia, which after her death was diagnosed as Alzheimer's. There were times when she said the most outrageous things. Though she never said people went missing, what if she had? I wonder if I would have believed her the way Kris had believed Sadie. I'd like to think so.

And since Kris needed someone to help her, it seemed only fitting to bring Gabe Burke back into her life. Gabe first appeared in my February 2007 book titled *Double Deception,* the first of the McClain series. I had always intended to make him the hero of his own story and this seemed the perfect one. I hope you enjoyed reading about their reunion and romance amid the mystery of the missing residents.

Keep an eye out for Angie's story in *Covert Pursuit* coming soon.

Blessings,

QUESTIONS FOR DISCUSSION

1. What made you pick up this book to read? Did it live up to your expectations?

2. Did you think Kris and Gabe were realistic characters? Did their romance build believably?

3. Talk about the secondary characters. What did you like or dislike about the people in the story?

4. Was the setting clear and appealing? Could you "see" where the story took place?

5. If someone you loved told you people were disappearing, would you be as willing as Kris was to believe?

6. Do you have a grandparent or elderly person in your life? How have they helped or hindered you?

7. Even as an adult, Kris felt the parental bond was constricting and she made assumptions based on the past, but in the end she matured enough to see them as people rather than just her parents. What kind of relationship do you have with your parents? When did you finally see them as people rather than just parents? What does the Bible mean when it says to honor thy mother and father?

8. Gabe declared he couldn't believe in anything that he couldn't see or touch. But the Bible describes faith as being sure of what we hope for and certain of what we do not see. It took God answering Gabe's prayer in a tangible way for Gabe to accept faith. How did you come to your faith in God? Has God answered your prayers in tangible ways?

9. Did the suspense element of the story keep you guessing? Why or why not?

10. Did you notice the scripture in the beginning of the book? What application does it have to your life?

11. Did the author's use of language/writing style make this an enjoyable read? Would you read more from this author?

12. What will be your most vivid memories of this book? What lessons about life, love and faith did you learn from this story?

Here's a sneak peek at "Merry Mayhem"
by Margaret Daley,
one of the two riveting suspense stories in the
new collection CHRISTMAS PERIL,
available in December 2009 from
Love Inspired Suspense.

"Run. Disappear… Don't trust anyone, especially the police."

Annie Coleman almost dropped the phone at her ex-boyfriend's words, but she couldn't. She had to keep it together for her daughter. Jayden played nearby, oblivious to the sheer terror Annie was feeling at hearing Bryan's gasped warning.

"Thought you could get away," a gruff voice she didn't recognize said between punches. "You haven't finished telling me what I need to know."

Annie panicked. What was going on? What was happening to Bryan on the other end? Confusion gripped her in a choke hold, her chest tightening with each inhalation.

"I don't want," Bryan's rattling gasp punctuated the brief silence, "any money. Just let me go. I'll forget everything."

"I'm not worried about you telling a soul." The menace in the assailant's tone underscored his deadly intent. "All I need to know is exactly where you hid it. If you tell me now, it will be a lot less painful."

"I can't—" Agony laced each word.

"What's that? A phone?" the man screamed.

The sounds of a struggle then a gunshot blasted her eardrum. Curses roared through the connection.

Fear paralyzed Annie in the middle of her kitchen. Was Bryan shot? Dead?

The voice on the phone returned. "Who's this? Who are you?"

The assailant's voice so clear on the phone panicked her. She slammed it down onto its cradle as though that action could sever the memories from her mind. But nothing would. Had she heard her daughter's father being killed? What information did Bryan have? Did that man know her name? Question after question bombarded her from all sides, but inertia held her still.

The ringing of the phone jarred her out of her trance. Her gaze zoomed in on the lighted panel on the receiver and saw the call was from Bryan's cell. The assailant had her home telephone number. He could discover where she lived. He knew what she'd heard.

"Mommy, what's wrong?"

Looking up at Jayden, Annie schooled her features into what she hoped was a calm expression while her stomach reeled. "You know, I've been thinking, honey, we need to take a vacation. It's time for us to have an adventure. Let's see how fast you can pack." Although she tried to make it sound like a game, her voice quavered, and Annie curled her trembling hands until her fingernails dug into her palms.

At the door, her daughter paused, cocking her head. "When will we be coming back?"

The question hung in the air, and Annie wondered if they'd ever be able to come back at all.

* * * * *

Follow Annie and Jayden as they flee to Christmas, Oklahoma, and hide from a killer—with a little help from a small-town police officer.

Look for CHRISTMAS PERIL by Margaret Daley and Debby Giusti, available December 2009 from Love Inspired Suspense.

REQUEST YOUR FREE BOOKS!
2 FREE RIVETING INSPIRATIONAL NOVELS
PLUS 2 FREE MYSTERY GIFTS

YES! Please send me 2 FREE Love Inspired® Suspense novels and my 2 FREE mystery gifts (gifts are worth about $10). After receiving them, if I don't wish to receive any more books, I can return the shipping statement marked "cancel". If I don't cancel, I will receive 4 brand-new novels every month and be billed just $4.24 per book in the U.S. or $4.74 per book in Canada. That's a savings of over 20% off the cover price. It's quite a bargain! Shipping and handling is just 50¢ per book.* I understand that accepting the 2 free books and gifts places me under no obligation to buy anything. I can always return a shipment and cancel at any time. Even if I never buy another book, the two free books and gifts are mine to keep forever.

123 IDN EYM2 323 IDN EYNE

Name   (PLEASE PRINT)

Address   Apt. #

City   State/Prov.   Zip/Postal Code

Signature (if under 18, a parent or guardian must sign)

Mail to Steeple Hill Reader Service:
IN U.S.A.: P.O. Box 1867, Buffalo, NY 14240-1867
IN CANADA: P.O. Box 609, Fort Erie, Ontario L2A 5X3

Not valid to current subscribers of Love Inspired Suspense books.

Want to try two free books from another series?
Call 1-800-873-8635 or visit www.morefreebooks.com

* Terms and prices subject to change without notice. Prices do not include applicable taxes. Sales tax applicable in N.Y. Canadian residents will be charged applicable provincial taxes and GST. Offer not valid in Quebec. This offer is limited to one order per household. All orders subject to approval. Credit or debit balances in a customer's account(s) may be offset by any other outstanding balance owed by or to the customer. Please allow 4 to 6 weeks for delivery. Offer available while quantities last.

Your Privacy: Steeple Hill Books is committed to protecting your privacy. Our Privacy Policy is available online at www.SteepleHill.com or upon request from the Reader Service. From time to time we make our lists of customers available to reputable third parties who may have a product or service of interest to you. If you would prefer we not share your name and address, please check here. ☐

LISUS09

Love Inspired®
SUSPENSE

TITLES AVAILABLE NEXT MONTH

Available December 8, 2009

CHRISTMAS PERIL by Margaret Daley and Debby Giusti

Together in one collection come two suspenseful holiday stories. In "Merry Mayhem," police chief Caleb Jackson is suspicious when a single mother flees with her child to Christmas, Oklahoma, where danger soon follows them. In "Yule Die," a medical researcher discovers her patient is her long-lost brother—with a determined cop on his tail.

FIELD OF DANGER by Ramona Richards

Deep in a Tennessee cornfield, April Presley witnesses a grisly murder. Yet she can't identify the killer. Until the victim's son, sheriff's deputy Daniel Rivers, walks her through her memory—and into a whole new field of danger....

CLANDESTINE COVER-UP by Pamela Tracy

You're not wanted. The graffiti on her door tells Tamara Jacoby someone wants her out of town. Vince Frenci, the handsome contractor she hired to renovate the place, wants to protect her. But soon they discover that nothing is as it seems...not even the culprit behind the attacks.

YULETIDE PROTECTOR by Lisa Mondello

Working undercover at Christmastime, detective Kevin Gordon is "hired" to kill a man's ex-wife. Yet the dangerous thug eludes arrest and is free to stalk Daria Carlisle. Until Kevin makes it his job to be her yuletide protector.

LISCNMBPA1109